MAGIC IN OUR HEARTS

Magic in Our Hearts

A Novel

Jeanne McCann

iUniverse, Inc.

New York Lincoln Shanghai

Magic in Our Hearts

iUniverse books may be ordered through booksellers or by contacting:

iUniverse
2021 Pine Lake Road, Suite 100
Lincoln, NE 68512
www.iuniverse.com
1-800-Authors (1-800-288-4677)

This is a work of fiction. All of the characters, names, incidents, organizations, and dialogue in this novel are either the products of the author's imagination or are used fictitiously.

ISBN-13: 978-0-595-42899-1 (pbk)
ISBN-13: 978-0-595-87236-7 (ebk)
ISBN-10: 0-595-42899-1 (pbk)
ISBN-10: 0-595-87236-0 (ebk)

Printed in the United States of America

To the Twenty Year Club …

Annie and Mar, Helen and Toni, and Ms. P.

It is amazing that we're all going strong after twenty years—it isn't just magic!
Here's to twenty more!

Acknowledgements

Thanks for the encouragement from family and friends and to Toni's editing skills, your support makes writing so much more fun.

This was an interesting book to write after experiencing knee replacement surgery. The recovery was a life-changing event and I was glad to be able to illustrate it in this story.

CHAPTER 1

▼

"God, Jeb, I am so *not* enjoying my life right now." An elegant woman in a stunning navy blue evening gown slouched lazily down on the stylish black leather couch. Diamond studs in her earlobes sent out fiery sparks each time she moved her head. Her posture was completely incongruous to her attire. She looked like she had just stepped off a fashion runway and collapsed.

Looking around the high-end condominium located in Brentwood, a suburb of Los Angeles where the movers and shakers lived, you could tell that the person who occupied the home was wealthy. Watercolors by local artists adorned the walls and lush off-white carpet stretched from wall to wall. The kitchen area boasted a Sub-Zero refrigerator and a Viking range, something one would expect to find in an upscale restaurant. The north side of the large living space was wall-to-wall windows with a view of the surrounding hills dotted with home after expensive home. Along with the plush leather couch, there were side chairs upholstered with a modern op art print containing blacks, blues and creams to match the blue lampshades. The room had been professionally decorated to match its owner, a highly sought after physical therapist to star athletes.

The other spaces in the condominium were similarly decorated, with the exception of the owner's bedroom. There, the stark style was replaced with opulence and deep jewel colors. The room, with its large four-poster bed, was swaddled in silk draperies and included a matching bed canopy in deep reds, striking yellows, and burnt orange. The walls were painted a rich goldenrod to add warmth to the sensuous sanctuary. The owner's true personality became apparent after noting the collection of colored bottles on the antique makeup table alongside various powders and creams. A hardback book by a popular romance novelist lay on the bedside stand, a testimony to the romantic soul of its reader. And Taylor was just that mix of practicality, style, and control, with a center full of romantic notions. She kept this part of herself well hidden except to those closest to her, and they were few. She was an extremely private woman who was fiercely loyal to her close friends. They were her family, and she loved them deeply.

"Honey, you have just about everything a girl could want." The tall, handsome, silver-haired man in a black tuxedo handed her a glass as he sat down next to her. The tuxedo was Armani, as was the shirt, expensive and well cut to fit the large-shouldered man. His silk pants hung perfectly on his tall frame, looking as elegant as the living room itself, not to mention its other occupant. They both would fit in comfortably at a movie premier, an exclusive club, or an A-list restaurant.

"I know, and I still feel lonely and lost. What's wrong with me?" The woman laid her head back against a supportive shoulder as she sipped from the glass of brandy.

"What's going on, Taylor? The business is good, you couldn't make any more money, and every time I turn around you're out with another gorgeous woman. What more do you want out of life?"

Taylor Aronson sighed as she looked back at her best friend and business partner, Jebodiah Beauregard III. She smiled and reached out to stroke his chiseled cheek affectionately. He was a gorgeous, caring man. His hair was a generous mane sprinkled throughout with silver. His lips were full and sensuous as he grinned back at her. Many a person had seen them together and commented on what a stunning couple they made. That observation couldn't have been more off base. There had never been anything sexual between them. Taylor and Jeb were both homosexuals and had been as close as two people could be since their second year of college. They had liked each other from the first moment they had met, and there was no one they trusted more than each other. They had stood by each other's side for several years and each considered the other to be family.

At the start of their second year of college, each of them were struggling to understand their emerging sexuality. Both were such handsome people that they were understandably inundated with unwanted advances from the opposite sex, yet each had no other person in whom to confide in.

It was at a large college fraternity party that they actually met for the first time. Taylor had been invited by an acquaintance from her anatomy class. She didn't know a lot of people at the school, and she accepted the invitation hoping to meet some other students. She had entered the frat house with some trepidation but found it crowded with college students who made her feel welcome. The place was wall-to-wall people in the run-down house, with beer kegs set up prominently in the back yard. She had pushed herself through the mass of loud and energetic people to help herself to a mug of beer.

Mike Sharpe was one of the few people she was acquainted with. He had been in her sociology course earlier that year and had immediately gravitated to Taylor, showing her unwanted attention despite her frequent rejections. She had refused numerous requests to go out with him using humor and honesty to rebuff his advances. She tried to avoid him at this party, but he zeroed in on her almost immediately and cornered her against a wall in the kitchen. Mike was a soccer player and a good-looking young man.

"Come on, Taylor, you know you like me. Why not go to the game with me tomorrow?" Mike teased, as he moved closer to her. In Mike's mind, there wasn't another woman in the room that could hold a candle to her. She was in stunning shape, worked out almost religiously, and her dark red hair and bright blue eyes were an unusual combination. Everyone noticed Taylor, and Mike wanted her more than any other young woman he knew. She was so aloof—friendly, but apparently shy—and she refused to go out with him. This was something new to him. Mike was a blond, blue-eyed man, with the stature and demeanor of a young Viking. He never had a problem with dating, or for that matter just hooking up. Girls had been easy for him since junior high—until Taylor, that is. She was a huge challenge and she was driving him crazy. The beer he had been consuming since early evening was adding to the problem. Mike was not a friendly drunk, and he was drinking more than enough beer to become completely hammered. Rejection and the alcohol fueled his temper.

"I do like you, Mike, but I don't want to go out with you." Taylor's voice softened as she spoke. She didn't want to anger the obviously inebriated man. She also didn't want to call attention to them and make a scene.

"Why not? I'll show you a really good time," Mike whispered, as he moved against Taylor, effectively pinning her against the wall with his body. He easily outweighed Taylor by a hundred pounds.

"Mike, leave me alone." Taylor shoved ineffectually against Mike's chest, her own temper flaring.

"No, I just want to kiss you." Mike demanded as he reached down and held Taylor's arms against her sides while he nuzzled her neck. Taylor felt panic well up inside her as she struggled against him. No one seemed to be paying attention to them, and she was beginning to be scared. She was usually pretty good at deflecting unwanted attention, but Mike was fueled with anger and alcohol.

"Hey, Mike. I think the lady wants to be let go." A deep voice spoke from behind Mike. Taylor couldn't see anything as she continued to struggle to free her arms. Mike's body completely covered hers as he pressed her tightly against the wall.

"What business is this of yours, you fuck?" Mike turned to find a tall man standing behind him. He stood close to Mike, his eyes locked on his face.

"It's mine when you're forcing a woman against her will." The remark was made quietly, but there was no mistaking the challenge.

Mike turned quickly, aggression boiling up as he moved to take on the intruder. Taylor pushed away from Mike in time to see the stranger duck Mike's fist as he tried to plant it in his face. As Mike prepared to try to hit him again, the tall dark-haired man rapidly took him to the ground with a leg sweep and a shoulder hold that pinned Mike to the floor. He had successfully used a martial arts move that had caught Mike completely unaware. He bent over Mike and spoke quietly and with complete authority.

"I suggest you don't bother this lady anymore. If you do, it will be me that you'll have to deal with instead of a woman who is half your size. There's nothing more disgusting than a man who tries to force a woman against her will."

"Get the fuck off me," Mike snarled.

"Quit being an ass." The man stood up slowly and watched as Mike struggled to his feet, then sheepishly moved away. Her rescuer turned and smiled at a stunned and watchful Taylor.

"Are you okay?" he asked softly. His dark eyes were as gentle as his voice.

"Yes, I … I've never seen anyone move like that. I'm sorry you had to witness that ugliness." Taylor blushed with embarrassment as she apologized.

"The only person who should apologize is the jerk that wouldn't leave you alone." The man smiled down at Taylor as he spoke quietly to her.

"Well, I really appreciate your help. My name is Taylor."

"My name is Jeb."

"Can I get you a drink Jeb?" Taylor grinned up at her savior.

"Sure."

That was the start of their friendship. It didn't take either of them long to admit to the other that each was homosexual. It also helped when they went out together because people naturally assumed they were dating and left both of them alone. This pleased both Jeb and Taylor because it allowed them to keep their private lives separate, something they both valued highly. Jeb and Taylor were both trying to understand their attraction to their own sex and spent many hours talking with each other about their feelings.

The friendship had grown and strengthened to the point where they considered each other family. Becoming business partners had followed naturally.

Jeb smiled at the incredibly beautiful woman who looked back at him. He loved Taylor without reservation, and she had supported him and been by his side for over fourteen years, never wavering in her love. He had given her many reasons to abandon him. Even when his wealthy family had thrown up their proverbial hands and cut off his money his last year of college, she had shared what little she had with him. After he had drunk himself nearly to death, she had bundled him into her broken down Volkswagen and driven him to the hospital. Coming out as a "fag," the term his father and brothers used to refer to Jeb, had been difficult for him. He was the oldest son of a wealthy family from Savannah, Georgia, and used to having everything that money could buy—everything but family acceptance. They were disgusted and ashamed of him and thought the best way to punish him was to cut off his access to the family money and deny his existence. He hadn't spoken to a single relative since the fateful day he had been confronted by his father. That was a memory he chose to bury, the heartbreak deeply embedded in his soul. He missed his family very much, but he knew without a doubt he could live only by being true to himself. Jeb credited Taylor's love and support for getting him through college with a business degree and his sanity intact. She had attended night after night of AA meetings with him, as he struggled to keep from falling deeper into the bottle. Now, he had been sober for almost thirteen years, and he was stronger than ever in his resolve never to let alcohol destroy his life. He still attended meetings whenever he needed additional support. It would be a lifelong struggle.

Taylor took one more sip from the cut crystal glass and watched Jeb sitting quietly next to her. He was such a gentle and loving person. "You'd better call Rex. He'll be worried about you."

"He knows I'm here, and he's too busy to miss me," Jeb responded, placing his large hand gently against Taylor's cheek. Taylor's looks had always been so amazing, with her red hair and pale blue eyes. Hers was not the red that came with a sprinkling of freckles, but was the deep dark red of cherry wood, thick, sleek, and straight to her shoulders. She stood all of five feet four without heels on, and her body was voluptuous and strong. Taylor prided herself on staying in superb shape, not only because her profession required it, but also because it was important to her. She worked extremely hard to maintain her well-toned body. "I saw you with Sadie. Why didn't you take her up on her apparent offer?" Jeb grinned, as Taylor looked back at him with a smirk of her own.

"She was pretty obvious, wasn't she? There's nothing subtle about Sadie."

Taylor had found Sadie Lawrence's pursuit of her flattering, and she had almost succumbed to her persistent attentions. It was no secret that Sadie wanted desperately to sleep with Taylor. Taylor had felt her body heating up as Sadie ran her fingers down her shoulder while they had stood quietly talking earlier that evening. Jeb and Taylor had attended a charity fundraiser put on by the local chamber of commerce. The charity, for handicapped and physically challenged children, was one that both Jeb and Taylor supported. In her work as a physical therapist, Taylor had occasionally worked with some of these same children. It was work that filled her heart as well as broke it, at times. Sadie Lawrence was a local newscaster for a morning news show that covered regional events. She was beautiful, intelligent, and indiscriminate in her pursuit of desirable women. Taylor had met her several years earlier while working with a famous male tennis star with a horribly damaged shoulder. He had attracted a lot of media attention due partly to his standing as the second best male tennis player in the world. He also attracted a lot of attention to his bold in-your-face lifestyle as a rich playboy. Sadie had been one of the many newscasters who had vied for his attention. She was ruthless in her pursuit of the golden boy and had successfully gotten him to agree to an interview while working out at Taylor and Jeb's facility. Having no objection to free advertising, they had agreed, and Sadie and her team had descended on the business like a platoon of infantrymen. For over four hours, she had interviewed the sexy and wildly entertaining athlete. He was not shy about giving credit to Jeb and in particular, Taylor, for his recovery. Sadie had taken one look at the physical therapist, whose looks alone could garner her a modeling career, and she was in hot pursuit. Not known for being hesitant in her pleasure seeking, Sadie became convinced that she had to sleep with Taylor, no matter what Taylor wanted. Arrogance was one of Sadie's strongest personality traits. She was a brilliant and beautiful woman who thought it was her due to sleep with anyone who was the least bit appealing. Taylor found her cavalier behavior disturbing and wanted nothing to do with the vivacious and determined newswoman. She was physically attractive, and Taylor couldn't help but respond to her, but she would not sleep with her.

"Why are you here alone?" Jeb asked, as he gazed back at his friend. "There's nothing wrong with a little consensual sex."

"That kind of sex just makes me feel so empty. I want to be with someone who doesn't view me as a notch on her belt."

Taylor's looks generated a lot of attention. The fact that she and Jeb ran a very successful sports medicine clinic and spa made her a very popular woman. And Taylor did like the ladies—a lot. "Besides, I just wasn't in the mood."

Jeb accepted the comment with a nod, but he knew there was more to it and he waited Taylor out. He knew that she would share her feelings in her own good time.

"Jeb, it just didn't seem right to go home with Sadie. I don't want to have a relationship with her." Taylor spoke softly, as she gazed up at Jeb.

"Since when has that stopped you?" Jeb knew that Taylor didn't sleep around a lot, but she was known to enjoy a casual sexual relationship with an attractive woman.

"I'm sick and tired of dating a woman once or twice and sharing a couple of nights of sex, then nothing more. I want what you and Rex have."

"Honey, you *will* find someone." Jeb knew Taylor's innermost thoughts. She had lost both parents while in high school, and ever since college Rex had been her only family. Taylor wanted a family of her own, a woman to love, and a couple of kids. It was something she spoke about quite often.

"How will I do that? The only women I come in contact with are athletes—arrogant, egotistical athletes." Taylor's opinion of them was mirrored on her beautiful face. Many of the finest and most well known athletes came to Taylor because of her skills as a physical therapist. Her close contact with them didn't make her one of their fans. Taylor understood that arrogance was a large part of the reason most of them were world-class athletes. She didn't have to like it, though.

"They seem to like you an awful lot, and they especially like what you do for them."

"I know. I just want to meet someone who looks forward to more out of life than the next tennis or golf match." Taylor laid her head against Jeb's shoulder. "What's wrong with me?"

"You need some passion in your life, honey."

"And how do you suggest I find that?"

"You might need to take some chances, honey. It means you have to love someone no matter what, and believe with your heart that they will love you back. Taylor, you can't only be with women you can control." Jeb spoke honestly. Taylor's one fault in her relationships was that she chose women that she could easily manipulate.

"I don't control anyone," Taylor protested quietly, but she knew Jeb was right. She did pick women that she knew she could persuade to her way of thinking. "I'm just so tired of work right now."

Jeb glanced down and smiled as he looked at Taylor's lovely face now scrunched up into a pout. She was a champion pouter. "Well, something came across my desk last week, and I was about to send the request to another clinic. Maybe you should hear about it."

"What is it?" Taylor looked up at Jeb with renewed interest.

Normally, Jeb ran the business end of the clinic and spa and Taylor took care of the hiring and training. Taylor was a board certified physical therapist and sports trainer and was well known for her ability to rehabilitate injured athletes. In fact, her reputation was widely renowned and respected in spite of that fact that she was a stern and demanding taskmaster who expected her clients to work hard. In return, she developed programs that gave her clients much more than hope. Taylor's regime of total fitness returned them to the world they lived for, the world of sports. And there was no shortage of famous athletes with injuries that threatened their livelihood. The business was lucrative and bursting at the seams with clients.

"Mrs. Camden, the matriarch of a wealthy family in Boulder, Colorado, contacted me last week with somewhat of a unique request." Jeb had spoken at length to Mrs. Camden. He had not, until that moment, let Taylor know about the unusual request. He knew the effect it would have on Taylor, and he didn't want to see his best friend hurt in any way. He would protect Taylor from anything that could harm her but he now realized that it was exactly what she needed.

"What?"

"It seems that her only child, a young woman, was terribly injured while skiing. Her legs were broken in several places, her knees had to be replaced, and her left arm was badly crushed. She's undergone seven surgeries and is now going through painful physical therapy."

"What's the request?"

"She wants to hire a physical therapist with sports training experience to help her daughter recuperate. She wants this therapist to commit to a six-month time frame, and she wants the therapy to be exclusive to her daughter. She's willing to pay and pay well." Jeb didn't mention to Taylor that Mrs. Camden had a personal reason to hire her, beyond Taylor's stellar reputation, and had wanted to speak directly to Taylor. In truth, she was the only physical therapist that Mrs. Camden wanted for the job.

"We don't do that."

"I know, but I think this job might be right up your alley." Jeb looked at her, his eyes serious. He expected once Taylor understood the request, she would not say no.

Taylor was intrigued. "Why?"

"You know the daughter. She was a world-class downhill racer and a well-known party girl, Brett Andreson."

Taylor's head snapped around as she heard a name from her past. "I didn't know she was hurt. I just assumed she had stopped racing."

"The information about her injuries was intentionally kept quiet because of the circumstances surrounding her accident. She and another woman were partying quite heavily at the family home in Boulder when they decided to go skiing. Brett was showing off on the downhill slope and lost control, slamming into a tree. That was nine months before the 2002 Winter Olympics. She was to be the shining star of the U.S. Ski Team. Her injuries were devastating."

"I do remember noticing she wasn't skiing anymore. I just thought she'd grown bored with it." But Taylor knew in her heart that there must have been more than simple boredom that led to Brett's disappearance from skiing and the Olympics. Brett's lifelong dream had been to ski in the Olympics. Taylor just hadn't wanted to know anything about Brett. It hurt too much to dredge up the past.

"I saw her medical records, Taylor. She was lucky to live through the accident. She was in a private hospital for almost four months. The surgeries she went through must have been excruciating." Jeb watched Taylor carefully. He knew how much she had grieved when the one serious relationship that Taylor opened her heart to had blown up in her face. She had mourned for over a year, never quite healing from the breakup.

"That all happened over two years ago. Why is her mother looking for a live-in physical therapist now?"

"The last one quit, and she wants her daughter to be more self-sufficient." Taylor gazed up into Jeb's face and waited. She knew that there was more. "Mrs. Camden has been diagnosed with advanced lung cancer and has only months to live."

"Oh, my God! That will destroy Brett. She loves her mother more than anything." Taylor's mind flooded with memories of Brett Andreson, a woman she hadn't seen or spoken to in over six years. Brett may have been a party girl but her family, especially her mother, had always come first. Jeb sat back and waited, his eyes watching the play of emotions on Taylor's beautiful face. She could hide nothing from him. He was one of the few people who knew that Brett had broken Taylor's heart so many years earlier and left her questioning her ability to ever have a successful relationship.

CHAPTER 2

▼

After college, Jeb and Taylor's business had started slowly with a big dream and a small office in Los Angeles. As the two of them networked and connected with other physical therapists in the area, Taylor started to make headway with her unique and well–planned program for injured athletes. She called it *the mind and body program*, being a firm believer that without a positive mindset and healthy lifestyle, recovery would take longer and be less successful. The first four years they barely paid the rent on the two-bedroom apartment over their tiny clinic, but they loved every minute of the struggle. Working long hours, with little more than the bare essentials, they had flourished, building their reputation and their clientele one success at a time. And they supported each other in every way.

It had been Taylor's connection with the sports teams in the area that had brought in several clients with serious injuries. Taylor's successes created more interest and generated more clients, which meant the business needed a larger space and more employees. It was Jeb's head for business that allowed him to design and develop the business plan for the clinic and spa as it was today. They called it "The Mind and Body Clinic and Spa." Over the years the business had grown to encompass a staff of forty-three and had a yearly income in the millions. This was primarily due to the endorsements of many professional and well-known athletes who had successfully used their services. Taylor had assisted in the recovery of many famous athletes after potentially career-destroying injuries. These clients had paid her back by establishing her reputation and recommending her to other athletes. The spa was the first place world-class athletes thought of when they needed to recover from potentially career ending injuries.

Jeb and Taylor found themselves making more money than they knew what to do with as more and more clients showed up on their doorstep. Their success had provided them with nice salaries, and Jeb had bought a house of his own while Taylor purchased a high-end condominium. Along the way, they had enjoyed being single and carefree in swinging Los Angeles, until four years earlier when Jeb had met and fallen in love with Rex Bonn, a talented chef at a local restaurant in Hollywood.

Rex's eatery had raised the bar for restaurants with fresh and nouveau cuisine and catered to the fast moving and discerning Hollywood crowd. Even the name reflected Rex's philosophy as a restaurateur. He had called his restaurant *Fast* because of the fact that he changed his menu monthly to keep the interest of the wealthy people who patronized his business and to define his quick rise to success from head chef of another restaurant to owner. He had decorated *Fast* in a minimalist style, expecting the food and the clients to be the main attractions. He wasn't wrong. With grey, black, and red as the only colors used throughout the place, he had struck gold with the atmosphere, not to mention the cuisine. His place attracted the famous, the wealthy, and a large population of gays and lesbians to the hot spot. It was a place to be seen in a city that boasted many a fine restaurant. Reservations were made weeks in advance and were highly sought after.

Jeb and Taylor had gone to the restaurant for dinner one evening to meet a potential client from the PGA golf circuit. Rex, as he was known to do, spent time visiting with all of his guests, stopping at each table to welcome them. Rex was not only a talented chef but had a rapier wit and a wicked sense of humor. When he arrived at Jeb and Taylor's table, he proceeded to tease the professional golfer and make Taylor laugh with abandon. But it was his hazel eyes that captured Jeb's attention, as they gazed at him appraisingly and with obvious appreciation. Jeb thought Rex was one of the most beautiful men he had ever met with his generous smile and ready laugh. Rex had looked Jeb right in the eye and asked if he wanted to attend a wine tasting party with him the following evening. With a grinning Taylor watching with interest, Jeb had blushed and agreed to go. Jeb was known to date but not often. He was selective in his choice of men, but Rex was different and Jeb had been hooked from that first moment.

It had been love at first sight, and the two men had eventually settled into a comfortable relationship that included Taylor as part of their family. It was understood that they would include Taylor in their small family. With essentially no other family to turn to, this had worked well for all concerned. Within two months the men were cohabitating and enjoying life as a couple. Rex worked nights at his restaurant and during the day developed new dishes to introduce to his discriminating clientele. Jeb always joked that he had gained twenty pounds the first two months they were together. Taylor spent many a night eating dinner with Rex and Jeb at a back table in the private area of his restaurant, and Taylor grew to love Rex completely. He was a loving and hopeless romantic who wanted more than anything to find someone for Taylor. He was always seeking out women to introduce to Taylor, and much to her chagrin. Brett had been one of those women.

Brett Andreson was a charismatic woman, a talented athlete, and a major player in the greater Los Angeles area. Her coal black hair, dark eyes, and generous mouth were arresting, as was her strong, muscular body. Being the only child of a wealthy family, Brett never lacked anything, including a stable of women who were in and out of her expensive loft. She was easily bored and went through relationships quickly, making it clear that she wanted no commitments from anyone. The only thing Brett ever took seriously was her skiing, and there she excelled.

Brett was best at downhill racing and giant slalom, where her fearless style and natural abilities were put to the test. She set record after record on the World Cup ski circuit, and eventually her only remaining goal in life was to garner a gold medal in the Olympics. She partied hard off the course, but worked out compulsively to improve her skiing. Finally, she became so skillful that no one could touch her on the ski slopes. She had promised her mother that she would win a gold medal, and Brett never, ever broke a promise to her mother. Whatever it took, she would win the gold and present it to the woman she respected above all others.

Brett frequented Rex's restaurant because of the excellent food and the predominantly gay clientele. Rex liked Brett from the first moment he met her. She was open about her pursuit of sex and fun, but hidden deep inside the woman's heavily armored heart was the need to find the one woman who would love her unconditionally. She didn't want someone to love her for her money or her fame, just for herself. Rex saw more deeply into Brett than she was aware of. He recognized a lonely woman that wanted more than anything to find the one woman she could be with for the rest of her life, and he wanted that woman to be Taylor.

Taylor and Jeb went to the restaurant for dinner one evening because Rex had said he wanted them to try out some new dishes. His true plan, however, was to introduce the two women. Rex had invited Brett to his restaurant for a special meal that included a tasty venison filet. He hadn't expected her to show up with two women in tow, all three far beyond mildly intoxicated.

Brett entered the small restaurant with the flare that she was known for. Two women hung on either side of her, both attired in designer label eveningwear. Brett was wearing a pair of navy silk slacks and an off-white muscle shirt that showed her amazing physique to perfection. She was laughing, her head thrown back, her dark eyes flashing with humor and intelligence. No one in the restaurant missed the wanton sexuality exuded by the stunning woman. She moved like a sleek, elegant panther, her toned, muscular body evident in every step. Although oblivious to the attention she was attracting, she caught the eye of both men and women as she and her party threaded their way through the crowded space. "Reservations for Brett Andreson."

"Yes, Ms. Andreson, follow me, please." The maitre d' led her to a private table near the one that Rex had reserved for Taylor and Jeb and where they were now seated. His plan had been to introduce the two women and let fate take its natural course.

The threesome never separated as they sat down at the table, the two blond women draping themselves like decorations over Brett as she accepted their attentions as her just due. She didn't mind spending time with two beautiful women, neither of which wanted a relationship. They just wanted to spend an evening with the sexy and talented skier and have uncomplicated sex.

Taylor looked on as the charismatic, dark haired woman ordered a bottle of expensive champagne and sat back, allowing the two women to vie for her attentions. Taylor found the scene wildly entertaining.

Brett was having a good time with Alicia and Carole, two women who liked to hang out with the US Women's Ski team. They both were wealthy groupies, who loved to play with the larger-than-life skier. She glanced around the crowded restaurant, seemingly unaware of the interest she was attracting. Brett was used to getting attention. Her eyes landed on a petite woman seated at the table next to her. She had dark red hair, unlike any color she'd ever seen. She was talking quietly to a tall, handsome man as they enjoyed the plate of hors d'oeuvres sitting in front of them. Brett continued to watch, fascinated by the woman's hair, shiny, thick and straight to her shoulders. And then the woman turned and locked eyes with Brett. Stunning aquamarine eyes gazed back at Brett, and the woman smiled. That smile took Brett's breath away. She felt like she had been hit by lightning, and her heart thudded in her chest.

Brett grinned back at the gorgeous woman and pushed the two blonds away from her. She bent and whispered something to each woman. They grumbled audibly as they stood up, picked up evening bags and wraps, and prepared to leave. Brett was no longer in the mood to play with them. She sent the two women on their way with no more than a request for a taxi to take them home. Rex walked up to Brett's table as the two pouting women headed for the door of the restaurant, disappointed that Brett wasn't going to continue their party.

"Brett, girl, you look good!"

"Thanks, Rex. Looks like you have a full house."

"Yep, business is good. Brett, let me introduce you to my partner, Jeb, and our best friend, Taylor Aronson." Rex turned and gestured to the table where the stunning woman sat.

"Hello, Jeb, Taylor. It's a distinct pleasure." Brett stood up and approached the table. She flashed a grin Jeb's way before reaching out to clasp Taylor's hand in greeting. Her considerable charm was tuned up to full wattage as she gazed down at the redhead.

Taylor felt the flash of energy and heat as she looked up into the laughing dark eyes of the handsome woman. "It's nice to meet you."

"Brett, sit, sit. I'm going to bring out some more food for these two. I'm trying out some new dishes and they're my guinea pigs. Join them."

"I will, thank you." Brett sat down quickly next to Taylor, her laughing eyes locked on to Taylor's unforgettable face.

Taylor could remember that night like it was yesterday. The minute she had looked at the sexy, inebriated woman, she'd been hooked. Brett might have consumed a large amount of alcohol, but that didn't hamper her ability to charm. She had made Taylor laugh with her and tremble with arousal. Brett proceeded to regale Jeb and Taylor with stories of her skiing and travels. She was funny, articulate, and bent on capturing Taylor's attention because the minute Brett had met Taylor, she had known. Taylor was the woman she had been waiting for her whole life.

Brett had grown up with parents that believed in love and commitment. Her mother had been widowed when Brett was twenty-six after Brett's father had lost his life in a small plane accident outside of Boulder, Colorado, while on a business trip. The loss had devastated the woman and her daughter was equally heart-broken. Both Brett and her mother grieved greatly over their loss. Robert Aronson had been a passionate and loving man who doted on his wife and daughter.

However, Roselin was not destined to live her life alone. She needed companionship and passion, and she had found both with her second husband. He was a calm and loving man who wanted nothing more than to live out his retirement taking care of her. With Brett's unqualified blessings, she had remarried two years after being widowed, and this marriage had also been a happy one. But fate delivered another cruel blow when Brett's stepfather suffered an unexpected heart attack within six months of his wedding date, shocking both Brett and throwing her mother into a severe depression. He had an undiagnosed problem with his heart, and at the age of sixty-three had passed away from a massive cardiac arrest. Roselin had lost not one, but two husbands she had cared for deeply. The commitment that Brett had witnessed in both her mother's unions was what she believed in and she wanted the same type of relationship for herself. But she had not met the woman she could commit to until that memorable night. The encounter rocked Brett's world. Taylor had been equally smitten. The evening proved to be an interesting and unusual encounter, but it was the week that followed that Taylor remembered most vividly.

Brett had pursued her with a vengeance. First, there had been beautiful orchids delivered to work in the morning and, for several days, amusing telephone calls just to chat. By Wednesday, Taylor had wanted to see Brett in the worst way and was surprised when Brett hadn't even suggested that they get together. By Friday afternoon, Taylor had figured Brett was off doing other things and not interested in anything about her, but Taylor had been very wrong. Brett had plans, big plans, and she was clearing her schedule and cleaning up her act. Her mother had suggested that she court Taylor and that was exactly what Brett was doing.

"Mind and Body Clinic and Spa, Taylor speaking."

"Hi."

Taylor didn't have to be told who was speaking. She immediately recognized Brett's voice. She flushed with attraction every time she heard Brett's voice. "Hello."

"How's your Friday going?"

"Good, thanks. How about yours?"

"Excellent. Would you be interested in going on a date with me?"

"It would depend upon when and what." Taylor was going to say yes no matter what.

"How about tomorrow? I thought we could go to the zoo." Taylor had been too shocked to respond. She would never have thought that Brett was the type of woman who would want to take her to the zoo. It wasn't something she expected from the worldly playgirl. "So, Taylor, what do you say?"

With a good deal more formality than she felt, Taylor responded, "Yes, that would be very nice."

"Good, I'll pick you up at your place tomorrow at nine. Have a great evening."

"Thanks, you too." Taylor hung up the telephone with a silly grin on her face. She had a date with a woman that fascinated her. She'd never felt quite like this before, but the feeling was exhilarating.

The date had been unique from the very start. They had wandered through the zoo all day long, sharing popcorn, hotdogs, and laughter. They had held hands in the darkened nocturnal animal house and touched frequently. They had talked almost non-stop for hours. Brett had brought her camera along and she had snapped picture after picture of the animals and Taylor. She had even asked a young man to take several pictures of the two of them together, her arm tightly around Taylor's waist.

By the end of the date, Taylor was in love, wildly and completely in love. But what cemented her feelings for Brett was the soft, glorious kiss that they shared on her doorstep. It had tugged at her already brimming heart as she was wooed by the gentle kiss.

"Brett, would you like to come in?" Taylor had known that if Brett touched her in any way she wouldn't be able to resist her, nor did she want to. She was overwhelmed with attraction for Brett.

Brett had nodded and smiled broadly while holding Taylor in her arms "Oh, yes, I would so very much, but I'm not going to."

"Why not?" Taylor was confused. She had thought Brett's attraction to her was obvious.

"Taylor, my usual behavior has been to sleep with a pretty woman and then immediately forget her name. I don't want to do that with you. I like you—a lot. I don't want to treat you like that." Brett had held Taylor gently as she spoke, her dark eyes locked onto Taylor's face. "Not that I don't want to make love with you. I do want you very much."

"I'm glad." Taylor's face had glowed with pleasure. "When can we see each other again?"

"Tomorrow—I'd like to see you tomorrow." Brett had brushed her soft lips slowly across Taylor's mouth in a gentle kiss.

"Good, that would be good," Taylor breathed, as she returned Brett's kiss. *God, the woman could kiss!*

"I'll pick you up at eight. Dress warmly." Brett brushed another quick kiss across Taylor's mouth and then turned and left her standing on her landing, surprise and pleasure on her face.

CHAPTER 3

▼

For the next three weeks Brett plied Taylor with romantic dinners, a surprise cruise on a sailboat, and quiet walks on the beach. She took her mother's advice to heart and was wooing the woman she planned to be with for the rest of her life. They talked about everything and shared their innermost thoughts and dreams. Taylor got to know the woman behind the athlete known to live her life large. They shared kisses and hugs until both women were ready to explode, but it was Taylor who decided when they would make love.

She invited Brett home for dinner, preparing everything from scratch. She pounded chicken breasts, chopped vegetables, and stirred sauce until she was ready to scream. Baking the caramel custard almost did her in, as she watched it cook in a water bath. She called Rex at least six times for his advice while fixing the meal. She wanted everything perfect, from the food to the meticulously set table for two. She arranged candles and used her favorite China, her best silver, and linen napkins artistically arranged on the plates. Rex chose the wine, and it sat on her counter breathing as she took one last look around the room before Brett arrived. She dressed carefully in a pair of teal blue silk slacks and a matching sleeveless sweater. Her hair was pinned up on the back of her head, and her feet were bare. She was nervously looking again at the table and jumped when the doorbell rang. Taylor took a big deep breath and went to open her front door. Brett stood grinning on her front porch, a large bouquet of iris in her hands. She was wearing a pair of black jeans and a white polo shirt, with leather moccasins on her feet. She looked like the sexy athlete she was, her dark hair loose and unruly around her beautiful face.

"Hi."

"Hi, come on in." Taylor stepped back to let her enter, her heart tripping loudly in her chest. This evening was so important.

Brett stepped up to Taylor and leaned into her, her dark eyes gleaming as she kissed Taylor softly in greeting. "I missed you."

Taylor's breath left her chest as she felt the impact of Brett's kiss and her words. "I'm glad you're here."

"These are for you." Brett handed the colorful spring bouquet to Taylor and glanced around the condominium. "I like your place. It looks like you."

Taylor started to enter the kitchen to put the flowers in water. She turned in surprise. "What do you mean?"

"Your place is elegant, stylish, and sexy, just like you," Brett responded, following Taylor into the kitchen.

"Thanks." Taylor blushed at the complement.

"Can I help with anything? The table looks nice."

"You can pour us both a glass of wine. Dinner is ready to be served if you're hungry."

During dinner, they laughed and chattered throughout the whole feast, which was delicious. Over after dinner brandies, the women were finally getting comfortable on Taylor's couch.

"Brett, can I ask you something?" Taylor spoke softly as she leaned against Brett. Brett's fingers were sliding through Taylor's hair.

"Sure."

"Will you make love with me?"

Brett's hand stopped stroking Taylor's hair. She was extremely nervous about her relationship with Taylor. She didn't want to screw it up. She was falling in love with her. "Are you sure?"

"Honey, I want to make love with you more than anything I have ever wanted," Taylor whispered, as her lips nuzzled the soft skin of her neck.

Taylor stood up, and Brett took her hand. Gently and slowly, she tugged her into the bedroom, her eyes dark with need. Brett stopped her at the bedside and spoke softly.

"I want you to know how important this is to me. I don't want this to be a casual relationship, Taylor."

"This is important to me, too. It's not casual for either of us."

Brett slowly removed Taylor's clothing until she stood naked in front of her. Her petite body was tautly muscled and yet feminine. Her breasts were full, her waist tiny, and her legs slim, the patch of red hair between her thighs as dark as the hair on her head.

"God, you are so beautiful, you make it hard for me to breathe." Brett gathered Taylor to her. "I'm so nervous."

"Why?" Taylor began to unbutton Brett's shirt wanting to run her hands over her superb body.

"This is our very first time and it's so important."

Taylor's heart thudded in her chest as she removed the rest of Brett's clothes. She gasped as she saw the strength and power of Brett's body. There was no question that she had worked hard at getting into shape. Taylor knew how much work it took to develop such a perfect body. It took dedication and conviction, traits that most people didn't recognize when they saw Brett. "Brett, this is special—what's happening between us."

"I know." Brett covered Taylor's mouth in a kiss, a soft full kiss that overwhelmed Taylor.

They moved onto the bed, their arms wrapped around each other, their bodies molding together. The contact of skin to skin made them both warm as passion built between them.

They made love tenderly this first time and memorized every inch of each other's body. Both women were overcome by powerful feelings as they touched and tasted each other, savoring their time together. It was a night of lovemaking that filled their hearts with magic and unexpected emotions. Brett trembled in Taylor's arms as Taylor feasted on her wet center, her mouth ravenous for the taste of Brett, and she held her tightly as Brett shuddered with an orgasm.

Taylor's eyes overflowed with hot tears as her body surrounded Brett's fingers that filled her completely and stroked her deeply until she exploded with pleasure. Brett's tongue tenderly captured her tears and held her as her body recovered. They made love long into the night until they fell asleep wrapped securely in each other's arms.

They spent every night together for the next two weeks, and they made love as often as possible. No words of love had been exchanged, but they were both in love, crazily in love. Nothing intruded on this magical and special time.

On a Wednesday several weeks later, Brett had to go out of town on a business trip for one of the ski team sponsors. Ski sponsors were the lifeblood of the program. It was their money that supported the many skiers on the circuit. She was scheduled to go to New York City for four nights with other members of the women's ski team. One night Brett was to appear at a cocktail party, one night was a charity auction, and another night was a sit-down dinner and benefit for pediatric aids. As part of the team, Brett had to attend a lot of publicity functions in order to represent the United States and gain sponsors for the team. Brett was adamant about not wanting to go out of town so early in their relationship and leave Taylor behind. She asked Taylor to go with her, but Taylor was swamped at work and couldn't get away. They'd made plans for when Brett was to return, neither woman anxious to be away from the other for even one night. The relationship was too new and too fragile and trust was just beginning to grow between them.

The first night they had spoken to each other five times on the telephone, spending an hour in one conversation that lasted late into the night, talking about anything just to hear each other's voice. The second night Taylor had lain awake for hours waiting for Brett to call. It was after one in the morning before the telephone rang.

"Hello."

"Hi." Brett's voice was full of exhaustion.

"How are you?"

"Tired and bored and I miss you." Brett was also getting fed up with dealing with the women that hung around the ski team wanting to be involved with a world-class skier. Her only thoughts were for Taylor and the relationship they were just beginning. She was no longer interested in frivolous, casual encounters. She wanted a real relationship with one woman, and that woman was Taylor.

"I miss you." Taylor wanted nothing more than to have Brett home with her. Until this trip, they hadn't slept apart in over two weeks.

"One more night and I'm out of here. I want to be with you." Brett had sounded almost desperate as she spoke.

"Is everything okay, Brett?" Taylor began to worry. She had a hard time believing that Brett wanted to be with her exclusively. Her reputation broadcasted exactly the opposite. Brett was famous for her playgirl behavior, and Taylor wasn't sure Brett wanted to give that up.

"Not exactly. I just hate all this stuff. It brings out the worst in people." That was an understatement. She had been inundated with women who wanted nothing more than to spend an hour or so with the famous skier. They tended to come out of the woodwork at these events. Brett had been known to take advantage of the situation until this trip. Now nothing could distract her from Taylor and their fledgling relationship. She would not screw this up.

"What do you mean?"

"There are always obnoxious groupies around and they're totally annoying." Brett hated the fact that women threw themselves at her, and for the first time in her life she wasn't interested in playing around. She wanted only to be with Taylor for what she hoped was the rest of her life. "God, I wish you were here."

"I wish I was too. Brett, I, I …" Taylor tried to utter the words but something kept her from finishing her sentence. She loved Brett, but saying the words aloud scared her to death. Taylor had never been in a relationship where she had actually told a woman she loved her. This would be the first.

"Honey, when I get back can we go away for the weekend, just the two of us?" Brett needed to tell Taylor how she felt, that she wanted to be with her for the rest of her life.

"I'd like that. But right now, you should get some sleep. Don't you have some kind of photo shoot in the morning?"

"Yes, at ten," Brett sighed. She was fed up with all of the publicity.

"Go to sleep, baby. I'll see you soon."

"Goodnight."

It wasn't until the following evening that Taylor's world changed. It started with a local news story about Brett and the photo shoot. There was a video of the ski team having their pictures taken, and it was very obvious that the woman interviewing Brett was enamored of her. Her remarks and her looks were blatantly noticeable. That by itself wouldn't have bothered Taylor if it hadn't been for the quick shot of that same woman in an evening gown standing next to Brett at the benefit dinner, her arm tucked under Brett's elbow. Taylor didn't want to jump to conclusions, but her heart was aching in her chest. They had no formal commitment to each other, but she had thought they had an understanding. It would kill her if Brett slept with anyone else. She waited until after two-thirty in the morning before calling Brett's cell phone. It wasn't Brett that answered.

"Hello." The voice was deep and sultry, and Taylor's heart pounded in her chest.

"Is Brett there?"

"She's busy right now. Could I take a message?"

"No, I'll call her another time." Taylor was devastated when she realized who had answered the telephone. It was the woman from the earlier interview. The telephone dropped to the bed as she fell back, her heart aching, tears streaming down her face. She should have known not to trust Brett with her heart. Now, it was too late!

"Jesus, Tracey, give me my telephone and leave! I don't want you here." Brett's voice lashed out. She was tired of Tracey's antics and following Brett to her hotel room was the last straw. Tracey had been making passes at her all night. Brett had avoided making a scene while at the event, but her subtle rebuffs hadn't discouraged Tracey's pursuit of her. Brett had a horrendous headache and all she wanted to do was go to sleep. Tracey would not give up.

"That's not what you said the last time you were in town."

Some months earlier, Tracey and Brett had spent an evening drinking and dancing at a local nightclub. This had been a prelude to a night of sex, uncomplicated sex, or so Brett had thought. But Tracey wanted another night with the gorgeous and talented skier and she wasn't shy about her feelings.

"Who was on the telephone?"

"I don't know, some woman." Tracey's dark brown hair was coming loose from her chignon, and her eye makeup was smeared. The normally elegant woman was looking a little overblown and used up. Brett could no longer remember why she had once found Tracey appealing. Taylor was the only woman she thought about.

"Get out!" Brett became furious. The only woman who would be calling her was Taylor. God, what did Taylor think? It would kill Brett to lose Taylor.

"Come on baby, you know we could have some fun," Tracey whispered, sliding her voluptuous body against Brett's.

"I don't want you! Now get out!" Brett pushed Tracey out of her room and grabbed her cell phone. She frantically dialed Taylor's number.

"Hello." Taylor's voice was hoarse from crying.

"Taylor, did you just call?" Brett could have died when she heard the anger and hurt in Taylor's voice.

"Yes, I'm sorry I bothered you."

"You didn't bother me, honey. I always want to talk to you. The woman who answered was Tracey Hernandez, an old acquaintance of mine. She's gone."

"I just called to see how the benefit went." Taylor wasn't sure what to think. Why would Brett have a woman in her room at that hour?

"Come on Brett, get off the phone and play with me." Tracey quietly slipped back into the room using the key card Brett had left on the desk and spoke loudly enough to be heard on the telephone. She didn't like rejection, and if Brett thought she could push Tracey away so easily, she was sadly mistaken.

"Tracey, get the hell out of here!" Brett turned and snarled at her, furious that she was interrupting her conversation with Taylor.

Taylor heard the conversation clearly and Tracey was making sure of that. "No baby, I'm going to make you very happy tonight."

"I don't want you here!"

"You always say that, but you don't mean it."

"Taylor, believe me this isn't what it seems. I'm going to get Tracey out of my room and call you right back." Brett was becoming frantic trying to get Tracey out of her room while explaining everything to Taylor. She had to make Taylor understand. She had done nothing to encourage Tracey. Their relationship was over long before Brett had met Taylor, and she wasn't about to let Tracey interfere with that.

"Brett, don't call, please." Taylor was too mixed up and hurt to talk to Brett anymore. Brett's usual behavior and reputation were rearing their ugly heads. Taylor couldn't deal with knowing Brett was with another woman, she just couldn't. There could be no other reason for bringing the woman up to her room.

"Taylor, please believe me, I only want to be with you," Brett cried, as she tried to make Taylor understand. And Taylor wanted so badly to believe Brett, but she couldn't get past her reputation as a playgirl. Taylor's silence was deafening to Brett. "You don't believe me?"

"I want to."

"But you don't. You don't know my true feelings?"

"I thought I did."

"You do. You're the only one who does." Brett had lost her heart to Taylor, and she desperately wanted her to believe in her. She had sensed Taylor felt the same way. Why was this happening?

"Goodbye, Brett." Taylor's throat all but closed up when she uttered her words. She loved Brett, but she couldn't trust her. They couldn't be together.

"Taylor, wait, listen to me, please! I can explain. It's not what you think." Brett heard only the dial tone after Taylor hung up.

Frantically, Brett tried to call her back but Taylor wouldn't answer her telephone or her cell phone. Brett would have to wait to talk to her in person. She could make Taylor understand. She had to. Brett was so depressed. She never quite felt she deserved to be as happy as she had been over the past few weeks, and Taylor's rejection was just what she had expected. A woman like Taylor couldn't love her. She didn't have anything to offer. She tried to rationalize taking Tracey up on her offer, what would it hurt? But she couldn't. Her heart wouldn't let her. Brett crawled into bed and cried herself to sleep, unable to do anything but ache over the mess that she found herself in. Taylor would understand, Brett would explain everything to her and she would believe her.

CHAPTER 4

▼

Brett tried for almost a week to get Taylor to talk to her so she could attempt to explain what had happened. Taylor was hurt and very angry, and she refused to speak to Brett at all. Brett finally gave up and left town for a month of training. She could not understand Taylor's total rejection of her. It was as if they had never been together. Taylor cut her off completely, refusing to spend even one minute with Brett.

Angry and hurt, Brett reverted to her usual behavior of hard drinking and frivolous one-night stands with the numerous women who were attracted to the wild and talented athlete. Taylor heard about her exploits, and she became even more adamant than ever that the brief time she and Brett had spent together had meant nothing to Brett. She buried her broken heart and became even more resolved to never let another woman that close again. She locked her feelings away and never spoke to anyone about Brett again. It was as if they had never been together, except for the deep-seated pain in both women's hearts.

"Taylor, Brett looks terrible. She's lost a lot of weight, and she can barely walk without crutches. She's also drinking quite heavily, especially since her mother told her about the cancer." Jeb spoke softly, his eyes on Taylor as she absorbed the information.

Taylor listened closely and tried to imagine what Brett was going through. She was such a proud woman, and she had been in superb physical shape. The injuries must have devastated her. "She must be terribly angry about her mother's illness. They were extremely close."

Jeb remained quiet, as Taylor grew contemplative, her eyes closed in thought. He hadn't been sure he was going to tell Taylor about the request until the moment he had come out with it. He knew that Taylor still loved Brett. He also knew it would take that deep love to help Brett recuperate. He was hoping that he had done the right thing. There was no question that Taylor would honor the request. Her heart had already decided. She just needed to hear herself say it out loud.

"I couldn't be away from work that long."

"Taylor, your staff is very well trained, you know that. We could make do without you for a while."

"I don't know if I could work with her." Taylor looked up into Jeb's understanding eyes.

"She needs you, Taylor. You know her better than anyone. She needs your talents to help her heal. You're probably the only one that can help her. She's hurting so deeply right now that you may be her only chance."

"She might not want me to help her."

"Her mother is hiring you, not Brett."

Taylor sighed and her eyes filled with tears. She spoke so softly that Jeb had to lean down to hear her. "What if I can't help her?"

"But you can. More than anything Brett needs to believe in herself again. She'll need a strong will to be able to deal with her mother's death and her own injuries. You more than anyone know what it takes to come back from such horrific physical damage."

And Taylor did. Jeb was the only other person who knew how badly injured Taylor had been her freshman year of high school. She had been riding in the car with her parents on their way to a gymnastics match when a speeding truck had sideswiped their car forcing it into a cement divider in the middle of the highway. Both of Taylor's parents had been killed instantly, and Taylor had incurred multiple back and pelvis injuries that kept her in the hospital for almost two months. She had spent another six months in painful rehabilitation at a rehab center. If not for the attentions of a talented and wise physical therapist, Taylor believed she wouldn't have survived. It was also where Taylor's dream of becoming a physical therapist took root. Ruth Sloan had taught her well, and had taken the orphaned, vulnerable young woman into her home. Ruth and her husband, Seth, had opened their hearts to Taylor and offered her safe haven. Childless, they had accepted Taylor as their own, forging a new family. They had never formally adopted Taylor but had considered her their true child. She had returned their love and had treated them as a second set of parents.

Ruth and Seth had long passed the age where they could have children and had resigned themselves to that fact. Taylor was a blessing to the couple. She had needed a family that would love her and protect her. Taylor had found them to be generous and loving and they helped her to survive. She stayed with them all through high school, and with their kind and loving natures they had allowed her to heal both emotionally and physically. It had taken Taylor almost two full years to completely recover from her injuries, both mental and physical, and then she focused on keeping her body in excellent physical shape. She had a goal, and nothing would deter her from being the best rehabilitation physical therapist she could be. Ruth and Seth had been her rock and family until three years earlier when they had passed away within months of each other. Taylor knew in her heart that one could not live without the other. She missed both sets of parents deeply. "I want to see the file before I decide."

"It's in my briefcase."

"You have it with you?" Taylor looked up at Jeb quickly.

"I wasn't sure I was going to tell you about it." Jeb stood up and walked over to where his briefcase sat on the counter. Jeb never went anywhere without his briefcase.

He quickly removed a file folder from the slim black case, returned to Taylor, and handed it to her. He turned away from her and went up to the large picture window that faced out on the city. He knew Taylor would be deeply affected by the contents. Taylor took a deep breath and then slowly opened the file and studied the medical description of Brett's body. She read of the multiple breaks of both femurs, complete knee replacements, six ribs and three vertebrae fractured, a massive concussion due to a severe fracture of the skull, and a crushed left forearm. The diagram of the body showing locations of all the injuries didn't bother Taylor. She was used to seeing this type of information, though she hadn't worked with anyone quite this badly injured before. She turned the paper over and her breath was slammed out of her chest when she saw the photograph of Brett. Gone was the woman whose eyes sparkled with humor and intelligence. She saw a woman with eyes dark and full of pain. It broke her heart to see the complete devastation.

"Oh my God!" Tears began to spill from Taylor's eyes. The proud and arrogant athlete was gone. In her place was a broken, haunted woman, whose skin hung on her bones. Deep, dark circles were under her eyes, and there was no sign of the superbly beautiful body that Taylor remembered. "Jeb ..."

Jeb reached the couch in two strides and sat down quickly gathering Taylor in his arms while she wept unashamedly—crying for the woman she had loved and who now looked as though she was hanging on by a thread. Taylor was shocked and angry that no one had been able to help her all this time. Someone needed to help Brett heal, and that someone would be Taylor.

"I'm going."

"I know."

"Does she know that her mother contacted us?"

"No, but her mother asked for you specifically."

"Why?"

"She didn't say, but she said that if you had any questions, she would fly here and speak directly to you."

"Why can't she call me?"

"She wanted to speak to you in person. When she first called, you weren't in the office, so I spoke with her. When she told me her request, I told her I wasn't sure you'd agree to take on the job. Taylor, I wasn't sure I even wanted you to know."

"Jeb, you can't protect me from everything." Taylor reached up and placed her hand against his cheek.

"I know that, but I know how deeply Brett hurt you, and I didn't want to see you hurt again. Her mother is a nice woman who's terrified that she will pass away before her daughter recovers enough to be able to take care of herself, and I knew if she asked you to help Brett, you would agree."

"What made you change your mind and tell me?"

"She needs you, honey. She has a chance if you can let your love for her help her heal. She's already lost so very much. I liked Brett very much and it breaks my own heart that she is in such bad shape. I know you of all people can help her."

"She may not want to work with me."

"She won't. You need to know that before you see her. She'll hate that it's you. She'll fight you every step of the way. You have to put aside all your hurt and anger with Brett and just help her."

"It's going to be the hardest thing I've ever done."

"I know." Jeb gathered his best friend close. He hoped he was doing the right thing. He alone knew how much Taylor had loved Brett. And he was betting on that love to help heal the badly broken woman.

CHAPTER 5

▼

The following week Taylor followed up with a telephone call to Mrs. Camden and after a brief conversation she agreed to meet with her. Mrs. Camden had flown to Los Angeles the very next day.

Mrs. Camden, I'm Taylor Aronson." Taylor watched as the tiny, well-dressed woman entered her office. Her hair was black with streaks of silver throughout. It was swept up into an elegant bun on the back of her head. Her suit was understated and elegant, slate blue in color. She wore matching high heels. Her jewelry was limited to a large diamond-covered gold band on her left hand and diamond posts sparkled in her ears. She was a softer, more feminine version of Brett. Taylor caught her breath when Brett's eyes looked back at her. The woman gracefully sat down in a chair across from Taylor's spotless desk.

"Hello, Ms. Aronson. I appreciate your taking the time to see me." Mrs. Camden reached out a dainty hand to shake Taylor's. Her observant gaze took in the large office space with the sleek black glass-topped desk with a streamlined computer monitor sitting on the left side. It was a professional and stylish office, with photographs of well-known athletes attractively arranged on three golden yellow walls. Behind Taylor was a wide window overlooking the business district of downtown Los Angeles. The view acted as a frame for the beautiful woman who sat in the high backed black leather office chair. Brett had described Taylor in detail to Roselin, and she was stunning indeed. Her pale blue business suit was professional, stylish, and sexy. She was everything that Brett had said she was.

"It's no problem. Please have seat, and call me Taylor. Can I get you anything to drink—water, latte …?"

"Taylor, then, and I don't need anything, thank you. My name is Roselin. I imagine you are curious as to why I asked for your help."

"Yes, I am."

With no preamble, Roselin began. "I've known about your relationship with Brett for quite a while. Brett was in love with you. She described you perfectly to me, and we had many long conversations about you. If there's anyone who can reach my daughter, it's you. To be quite honest, I think you are the only person who can help her." Taylor hadn't been expecting the blunt, to-the-point explanation. She sat back in her chair thinking about her response.

"I, I … it was several years ago, and we saw each other for such a short time," Taylor stammered, somewhat shocked at this revelation.

"My daughter has never forgotten you. She has photographs of the two of you in her room." Mrs. Camden looked directly at Taylor as she spoke. "Taylor, I know my daughter better than just about anyone. She has never kept a thing from me. She doesn't lie to me. I know how much you meant to her because she told me she would only love one woman in her life. That woman was you."

"We saw each other for just a little over a month." Taylor's hands shook as she folded them in her lap. She wasn't expecting such brutal honesty from Brett's mother.

"I know. I also know that you refused to see her after you thought she was unfaithful. Taylor, I know how Brett behaved. She was wild, uncontrolled, and drank way too much. She treated the women in her life as passing toys. That is, until she met you. I always knew that when Brett met the right woman she would settle down."

"I don't know what to say to you." Taylor's hand trembled as she pushed her hair back from her face.

Mrs. Camden smiled at Taylor's confusion. "The day you and Brett went to the zoo she called me and told me she had met the woman she was going to marry. Taylor, I've always known my daughter. She reminds me so much of her father. He was a wild and impetuous man who lived life to the fullest, but he loved me with a single-minded intensity. My daughter is exactly like him. One thing I know about Brett is that she would never tell me she loved someone unless she meant it. She told me she loved you. Another way she's just like her father is that when they love, they love completely and deeply for the rest of their lives."

"But she had another woman in her hotel room."

"Yes, but I believe my daughter. She's never lied to me. She told me she didn't sleep with her that night. She did say that they had slept together months earlier.

But after she met you, Brett said she didn't sleep with anyone else. I know what her reputation has been. She didn't hide anything from me. I believed my daughter absolutely when she said that she was in love with you."

"I can't do anything about that now."

"No, but I know you loved my daughter very much. Brett shared her photographs of you with me and I could see it in your eyes in every one. I'm hoping that those feelings aren't completely gone and that you can help her."

"What if she doesn't want my help?" Taylor's eyes were glassy with emotion.

Mrs. Camden relaxed in her chair now that she knew Taylor was going to try to heal her daughter. Taylor's face was so expressive that she was able to hide nothing. Taylor still cared deeply for Brett. "Oh, my daughter is going to make you miserable. She's going to do everything in her power to make you hate her. She's going to fight you every step of the way."

"Why would she want to do that, and why would I subject myself to that kind of abuse?" Taylor was charmed by Mrs. Camden's smile. It was just like Brett's.

"Because if she was indifferent to you, you couldn't help her, and you need to teach her how to channel her anger into energy. Her anger and frustration are not really about you. She has lost so much since her accident. Her whole life Brett dreamed about skiing on the World Cup Circuit and going to the Olympics. Through her own irresponsible behavior, she destroyed all of her dreams. She has endured seven painful surgeries, and months of recovery in the hospital. I honestly don't know how she survived that ordeal." Brett's mother grieved deeply for her injured daughter, and her face was etched with sadness.

"I'm so sorry. She didn't deserve what happened to her no matter what decisions she made. If I agree to work with her and she demands that I leave, am I to stay on anyway?"

"You're going to be working for me, not Brett. No matter what she says, you *will* stay. But it's you who'll have to deal with her refusal to do much of anything to help herself." Mrs. Camden's voice was firm and direct, and her expectations were crystal clear.

"Okay. If I agree to take this on, I'm going to ask for a few concessions." Taylor couldn't take on this challenge if she wasn't given complete control over the entire situation. That was the only way she could work and have any chance of helping Brett.

"Name them."

"I want to live in the same space with Brett. I can't spend just a couple of hours a day helping her and then leave. And we need to be left alone as much as possible. I also want to have control of her diet and meals."

"Done. When can you start? I don't have much time left, and I want to see my daughter healthy before I die." Mrs. Camden had hidden strength that now became evident. She would do whatever was necessary to save her daughter.

The statement was so matter of fact that Taylor wasn't sure how to respond, but it was the hint of pain in Mrs. Camden's eyes that made Taylor stand up and move directly in front of her. "I'm so sorry about your illness."

"I am too, because I'm probably going to miss seeing Brett get her strength and spirit back. She's the only family I have left, and I don't want to leave her in such pain."

"I'll do my very best, and I can start after this weekend. Do you want me in Boulder?"

"Yes. She has a house there and Brett has been living in it. I've hired a small staff to help her, a cook and a housekeeper, not that they've been able to help very much. Brett refuses to eat much of anything. She much prefers to drink. And her cleanliness leaves a lot to be desired." The words were uttered quietly. Anger and pain made them even more poignant.

"Will you be there?"

"Yes, but in a separate house. I'll honor all of your requests, but I would like to see my daughter occasionally."

"Of course."

"I'll make arrangements for your airfare and arrival. Is Sunday okay for your flight?"

"That's fine. When are you going to tell Brett that I've been hired?"

"I'll arrange for you to be picked up at the airport when you arrive and have you brought to my home. Then the two of us will tell her together."

Both women knew that the meeting was going to be extremely difficult for everyone, and Taylor was glad that Mrs. Camden would be there. She had no idea how Brett was going to respond.

"I'll pay you very well, and all food and expenses will be taken care of for as long as it takes." Mrs. Camden stood up and looked into the stunning blue eyes that she had seen in Brett's pictures of Taylor. Brett was right. Taylor was a beautiful woman, and it was obvious that she was still very much in love with Brett. That much Mrs. Camden knew. It pleased her no end.

"Thank you."

"I owe you my thanks. My daughter is slowly killing herself, and I don't have enough time left to help her. I know you can."

Taylor was hoping she could help both Brett and her mother. She would do everything in her power to improve things for both of them.

CHAPTER 6

▼

Taylor saw the sign with her name printed on it in large, looping letters as soon as she exited the airport. A uniformed chauffeur helped her into the town car and loaded her luggage into the trunk. The rest of her things were being shipped later in the week. She sat anxiously in the backseat as the driver announced that the trip would take a little over thirty minutes and then fell silent. Taylor was beginning to panic as she reconsidered what she had committed to do. She almost missed the beautiful city that they drove through. The city was clean and businesses sprawled out in an inviting way, but it was the mountains in the distance that caught her eye. They were covered with snow and their jagged peaks were majestic. She could see why Brett had found skiing so appealing. The mountains had a way of calling to a person. The streets were wide and the majority of the cars on the road were SUVs with ski racks on top. Taylor counted four ski rental companies in a two-block section of town, several quaint restaurants, and a large shopping mall. After traveling for almost a mile out of town they turned into a suburb of high-end homes. The houses were large and sat comfortably on manicured lawns. Ten houses from the entrance, they pulled into the driveway of a colonial style white house with black shutters.

"Ms. Aronson, I'm to pick up Ms. Camden and then we will we will have another twenty minute drive."

Taylor watched the chauffeur go to the door and then escort Mrs. Camden to the limousine.

"Hello, Taylor, how was your flight?"

"It was fine, Mrs. Camden. I like your city. It's very charming."

"It is unless it's overflowing with weekend skiers. Just getting to the mall can take an hour. Are you ready to go to Brett's house?"

"Yes, I am." Taylor shivered as she thought about Brett. She was also terribly nervous about confronting her again after so many years. She had been able to avoid her until this moment, and she knew the meeting was going to be painful. She also expected Brett to be furious.

Taylor was dead right!

"Get the fuck out of my house!" Brett slouched between her crutches, her hair long and shaggy, and her eyes dark, sunken pits in her face. The tee shirt she wore was wrinkled and soiled, hanging loosely on her frame. The sight of her former lover all but knocked the wind out of Taylor. She had to bite her lip to prevent herself from crying out loud.

"Brett, Taylor is here to work with you as a physical therapist. She's going to help you with your rehabilitation. "Brett's mother had remained calm as she faced her furious daughter.

"God damn it, Mother, how many times have I told you? I'm not going to get any better? Don't you get that? There is no recovery; this is the best it's ever going to be. And why her? I don't want her here!"

Brett railed at her mother. And then to Taylor, "Leave now! There's nothing you can do here."

Taylor was too shocked by her first glimpse of Brett to do anything but stare. The photograph she'd been shown couldn't compare to the actual sight of the woman. Brett was gaunt, her eyes dull, her hair filthy. She was wearing a pair of baggy, wrinkled sweats and a torn, dirty tee shirt. She leaned heavily on her crutches as her eyes shot bolts of rage at her mother and Taylor.

"Brett, won't you please try for me?" Mrs. Camden's softly spoken plea shut Brett's anger down completely.

Brett's eyes filled with tears as she walked awkwardly toward her mother, the crutches keeping her steady. "Mother, I would do anything for you, but no one can perform miracles. I did this to myself, and I have to live with it. I'm not going to get any better than this. I've accepted that, why can't you?"

Taylor held back her tears as she witnessed the scene between mother and daughter. There was no doubt they loved each other deeply. Mrs. Camden's hand reached out and stroked her daughter's cheek, her hand gentle against her daughter's face. "Brett, I love you so much, and I know you love me. Do this for me, won't you please? Just try it for a little while."

Brett could not refuse her mother. She asked so very little of her, and Brett did love her dearly. She was the only person Brett trusted. "For you."

Taylor had to turn away from them, choking back her tears. There was so much love between them and so much anguish.

"Taylor will be staying here with you while she works with you."

"No!" Brett screamed, as she swung away from her mother, her face once more dark with anger.

"I need to be here, Brett," Taylor spoke for the first time since her arrival minutes earlier.

Brett shivered as the familiar voice penetrated her Scotch-fogged brain. "I don't want you here."

"I know, but I need to be here." Taylor gazed into the dark, familiar eyes. There was no way she was going to walk away now. One look at Brett had renewed her resolve.

Brett stared long and hard at Taylor before slowly turning her back without speaking a word. That dismissive movement hurt Taylor more than angry words. It showed complete indifference to her, and Taylor felt the tears well up again, this time for a different reason. It took all of her composure to keep from weeping.

Mrs. Camden spoke calmly. "Taylor, I'll show you your room and then introduce you to Helen and Fran. Either one of them can get you anything you might need. Helen is an amazing cook, and she's prepared to make whatever meals you request. She and Fran have both been told that you're in charge. They'll take their orders from you."

Taylor listened, but her eyes were on Brett who stumbled out of the living room through a doorway and slammed the door shut. She finally turned and looked directly at Mrs. Camden. "She breaks my heart."

No other words could have shaken Mrs. Camden more than those. Her arms reached for Taylor and she hugged her tightly, knowing in her own mind she had done the right thing. She tenderly held Taylor as she cried. After a few moments Taylor pulled away and wiped her face clear of tears.

"Show me my room, please. I need to get started as soon as possible." Taylor straightened her shoulders and stiffened her resolve. She had a lot of work ahead of her if she was going to help Brett.

"This way, please."

Taylor carried her suitcase up a short flight of stairs to the second story and a large bedroom with connecting bath. The view from the window revealed a scene of magnificent snowy mountains. The back of the house had a lawn that stretched out about seventy-five feet where it butted up to scrubby trees and foothills at the base of the mountains. The room was spacious, the double bed covered by a down comforter in pale yellow with green sheets and pillowcases. It was a soothing room with a natural wood dresser and armoire. The walls were a soft green moiré, and colorful floral paintings adorned the walls. A small desk was placed just under the window so the picturesque view was perfectly framed.

"The telephone is on the desk and I've set up a separate line for you. There's also a data port for a computer, if you need one. The bathroom is through this door."

Taylor followed the gracious woman into a bathroom that took her breath away. It was marble with a glass-enclosed shower and a deep soaking tub. The room was done in the same soothing pale green and yellow colors, including the large, fluffy towels. Someone had done an impeccable job of putting the room together.

"This is a beautiful home."

"Thanks. Brett spent about a year designing and decorating it when I gave it to her."

"This is Brett's home?" Taylor was surprised.

Mrs. Camden smiled, a smile filled with pain and love. "Yes, she told me she was making a home worthy of a partner. Her plan was to fall in love and live here for the rest of her life."

"When did she do this?"

"Eight years ago. It stood almost empty after she finished remodeling. She said she didn't want anyone to live here until she found her soul mate. She didn't move in until after she was released from the hospital the last time."

Taylor's heart shriveled in her chest. "Then she's found someone?"

Roselin had to prevent herself from smiling when she heard the worry in Taylor's voice. "No. Brett no longer believes she deserves to be loved."

Taylor was once again overcome with sadness at how much Brett had suffered, how much she had given up. "I'm surprised she gave permission for me to stay here."

"She didn't. Brett will refuse me nothing. I'm afraid I tricked her into this arrangement."

"What do you mean?"

"I made her promise that I could hire one more physical therapist to work with her. I knew she would go along with me because of my illness."

"That's, that's …"

"Emotional blackmail and I would do it again if it will help my daughter heal." Mrs. Camden met Taylor's eyes directly. She loved her only child unconditionally.

"You didn't tell her it was me?"

"No, I did not."

"Why?" Taylor had to understand Mrs. Camden's actions.

"Because she would have refused."

"She may not work with me." Taylor flinched as if she'd been hit.

"She will. I have complete faith in you, Taylor."

"I hope you're right." Taylor had serious doubts as to whether she could get Brett to do anything with her. Her show of indifference toward Taylor had cut to the bone. She felt she would have very little influence over the physically and emotionally scarred woman. She wasn't sure how she was going to reach her.

"I am, dear."

CHAPTER 7

▼

Brett slumped down in her chair and tipped back the cut glass crystal tumbler as she swilled down the last of the Scotch. Seeing Taylor after all this time had inundated her with pain. She hadn't seen her for years, but she hadn't forgotten a single detail about her. She was furious that Taylor had to see her in this condition. She had kept everyone at bay, so no one knew how far along her self-destruction had gone. Now, the one woman she had ever loved was in her home, planning to work with her. How ironic was that! It was going to kill Brett being around Taylor.

Reaching across the dust-covered table, she grabbed the open bottle of Scotch and refilled her glass. The large room was dark and gloomy. The only light was from a single lamp next to the rumpled, unmade bed. It was a dark cave, one that Brett hid in and where she drank herself slowly into oblivion. The only thing that helped Brett get through her days was her drinking. She was in constant pain and her body was covered with scars. Even walking was difficult, and she had no reason to get better. Her mother was dying and she had no one else in her life. She felt the sting of unshed tears and a wave of self-pity as she remembered the look of shock on Taylor's face. She must have been totally disgusted by what she saw. Brett couldn't even look at her own body in the mirror. She had destroyed it.

"God, I can't do this anymore," Brett sobbed, as she laid her head down on the table and cried uncontrollably. She lamented lost love, lost opportunities, and her mother's imminent death. She wept until she fell asleep, in part due to the alcohol and her lack of food. Her unwashed body slumped against the table in restless slumber as she fought against the alcohol that barely anesthetized her from her pain and anguish.

While Brett slept restlessly, Taylor was introduced to both of the women who took care of Brett's home and was told that dinner would be served whenever she wanted since Brett didn't take regular meals. The two women were as different as night and day. Fran was tall and slender, with dark brown hair interspersed with grey. Helen was short and stocky, due largely to her incredible cooking skills and her healthy appetite. Her hair was mostly grey, peppered with a few light brown strands and tied up on her head in a casual knot. Both women were loyal to Brett and wanted nothing more than to help Taylor help her recover.

"What can we do?" Fran and Helen sat at the kitchen table with Taylor. Roselin had left her with the two women and promised to call Taylor later that evening.

"You can help me get Brett on a regular schedule of meals and exercise. She needs structure to help her get back on track. She also needs to stop drinking and get the alcohol out of her system."

"Good luck! She's usually drunk by midday, and she doesn't eat a thing." Fran remarked. She and Helen had all but given up trying to keep Brett from drinking.

"She will have to come around in time. Helen, do you mind if I work with you on some menus? I've found that good, healthy food, heavy on protein, helps with the recuperation." Helen was a sixty-year-old Welsh woman whom Taylor liked immediately. She lived in the house in separate quarters attached to the back of the kitchen. Fran did most of the housekeeping and went home to her husband at the end of the day. It was not difficult to keep the place spic and span, except for Brett's bedroom. She wouldn't let Fran or Helen into her room.

"I'll do anything miss, if you can get some food into that one. She's skin and bones and refuses to eat anything at all most days. When she does eat, she just picks at things. I've tried everything I know how to do."

"She'll eat," Taylor announced with determination. Brett was going to get better, even if it killed Taylor. She was firmly resolved about what she had to accomplish.

"Can you get her to let Fran clean that pit of a room she hides in? It's filthy, and the only time she lets us in is when her mother forces her to. It's a crime for her to live like this."

"She'll let you clean it. Brett doesn't know it yet, but I can be just as stubborn as she is," Taylor remarked, her blue eyes sparking.

"Good luck, Ms. Taylor. We love her and it's sad to see her drinking so heavily."

"How does she get her alcohol?"

"We pick it up with the groceries and things. If we don't pick it up she has it delivered or a friend will drop it off."

"As of today, no more alcohol is coming into this place. If she asks you to get any more, come to me. I'll deal with her."

Taylor hurried out of the kitchen intent on locating Brett and speaking directly to her. Fran and Helen exchanged grins as they watched her heading in the direction of what they called Brett's dungeon. They were expecting an imminent explosion.

"There are going to be some fireworks around here," Helen commented, as she watched Taylor wrench the door open.

"It's about time," Fran responded, as they both steeled themselves for Brett's tantrum.

Taylor entered the dim room and hesitated in order to get her bearings. It was obviously a room that functioned as a bedroom, entertainment, and workout room. It was also obvious that the fully functional gym was not being used. Dirty clothes hung off the weights, and there was a layer of dust covering everything.

The draperies were pulled shut, even though it was early afternoon, the beautiful view totally blocked. She saw the bottle of Scotch next to Brett's hand, as she lay slumped in a chair, her head on a filthy table. Taylor approached her quietly and realized that Brett was sleeping or passed out, evidence of tears on her face.

"Oh, honey what's happened to you?" Taylor whispered as she moved closer to the unconscious woman. "Brett, honey, wake up."

"What ... what," Brett mumbled as Taylor gently shook her, the smell of alcohol and unwashed body almost overwhelming her.

"Get up, honey. You're going to take a shower and get cleaned up, and then you're going to eat a decent meal."

The alcohol had taken its toll, along with the medications Brett took to manage her pain. Her words were slurred, and she was almost incoherent. "Why, Taylor, why?"

"Why what?" Taylor helped Brett to her feet and wrapped her arm tightly around her waist. She was shocked at how bony Brett felt.

"Why are you here? Why you?"

"Because I want to help you." Brett's eyes were barely open, and she leaned heavily against Taylor as they moved slowly to the bathroom.

"Why you?"

"Because I care about you."

"I love you, you know." The words were so soft Taylor barely heard them as she moved Brett into the shower. But Taylor's heart leaped at the quietly uttered pledge. There was a shower chair in the large open shower and she gently sat Brett down in it.

Taylor wanted to wrap her arms around the inebriated woman and just hold her, but she didn't. Her heart was too raw with emotion and she needed to get Brett cleaned up. "Stay here, honey, I'll be right back."

Taylor flew out of the bathroom and ran for the kitchen, startling Fran and Helen when she burst through the door. "I need both of you to help me. Fran, can you change the bed in Brett's room and clear out some of the dust? Helen, I need you to make some hot soup and toast. I'm going to get her cleaned up and get some food into her."

"We'll do it!" Helen responded, surprised at how quickly Taylor was taking charge.

"Thanks. I'm going to help Brett take a shower. If you could change the bed first, it would really help. I'm going to put her in bed as soon as she's clean."

Taylor ran back into Brett's room, fearful of leaving her unattended in her current drunken state for long, but Brett was still slumped in the chair, her chin resting on her chest as she slept.

"Okay, honey, let's get these filthy clothes off." Taylor started to remove Brett's tee shirt.

"Hey, leave my shirt alone!" Brett snarled, as she began to fight with Taylor.

"You can't take a shower in your clothes."

"Leave me alone! I just want to sleep."

Taylor put her hands on her hips and glared at the very intoxicated woman. "You're taking a shower! You stink! Now, you can keep the clothes on if you want, but you *are* showering!" Taylor's voice bounced off the marble walls.

"Shit, quit screaming." Brett put her hands over her ears.

Taylor glared at Brett and then reached out and turned the shower on spraying Brett's face and chest with water. Her clothes were soaked as she shivered under the icy spray.

"Jesus! God damn it! What are you trying to do, drown me?" Brett sputtered, as Taylor calmly turned the shower up to full power.

"Remove those filthy clothes."

Brett looked up through her bloodshot eyes and wet, matted hair and recognized the look on Taylor's face. She wasn't going away. "Okay, you get the hell out and I'll take them off."

"No."

"Yes, God damn it!"

"You will take everything off and scrub every inch of your body."

"Get the hell out!" Brett snarled as she started to stand up. "I can do this by myself."

"I'll be right outside if you need me." Taylor smiled sweetly at the ill-tempered woman.

Brett swore and mumbled under her breath, but she stood up and took her clothes off. She couldn't let Taylor look at her scarred, disfigured body. That would kill her. She slowly stepped out of her things, adjusted the temperature of the water, reached for the shower soap and began to scrub her body and her hair. It had been a long while since she had taken a full shower.

Taylor smiled as she stepped out of the bathroom and saw that Helen and Fran had opened the draperies and were busily cleaning the room. In the full light of day the room was even more dismal, as the sight of several empty Scotch bottles laid testimony to what Brett was doing to herself. Garbage overflowed the one wastebasket, and dirty clothes were piled up everywhere.

"Here, let me help." Taylor gathered up a stack of dirty clothes and followed Helen out of the room as Fran made up the double bed. "I need some clean towels for her bathroom."

"I'll show you where everything is," Helen remarked as she led Taylor to the laundry storeroom. "There are towels and sheets in this room."

"Thanks."

"We should be thanking you. Brett needs someone to penetrate her thick skull. We've been so worried about her."

"I don't know if I can do much more than try and get her to eat and exercise. And she has to stop all the alcohol. She needs to get all of it out of her system and start focusing on her rehabilitation."

"She's going to go through withdrawal."

"I know." Taylor looked into Helen's eyes as she responded. It was going to be an uphill battle. They were all going to have to work together as a team.

"Here are a handful of towels."

Taylor hurried back through the bedroom and into the bathroom just as Brett stepped out of the shower. The sight of all the scars on the once beautiful body made Taylor cry out. Brett's skin was pale, making the angry red scars stand out. Four-inch scars slashed over both kneecaps, and several long scars jaggedly crossed her chest. Her skin hung on her emaciated frame with no evidence of muscle tone in any part of her body. Her ribs were evident, and her stomach was concave. She looked half starved.

"Oh Brett …"

"Get the fuck out!" Brett screamed, mortified that Taylor was seeing all that she had done to herself.

"I brought you some clean towels," Taylor whispered, her eyes locked on Brett's angry countenance.

"Get out!"

Taylor backed quickly out of the bathroom before she burst into tears. The beautiful body she remembered was literally crisscrossed with surgical scars, evidence of the extensive work done to repair her body. Taylor grieved over the amount of pain and suffering Brett had gone through.

Brett picked up a towel and buried her face in it. Hot tears streamed from her eyes as she felt the shame and embarrassment deep in her heart. "Goddamn it, why Taylor?"

Taylor turned and found Fran and Helen watching her closely, their faces studies in compassion. "She's gone though so much."

"Yes, she has."

"Where are some clean clothes for her to wear?"

"In the credenza over there are sweats and tee shirts, along with underwear."

Taylor slowly went over and rummaged through the drawers, pulling out sweats, a shirt, and clean panties. She approached the bathroom door with trepidation, knowing how angry Brett was. She knocked softly on the door.

"What!"

"Brett, I have some clean clothes for you."

The door was ripped open and, before Taylor could utter a word, Brett grabbed the clothes from her and slammed it in her face. Taylor backed away and turned to the two grinning women.

"Well, that went well," Fran commented, as she turned back to the bed and finished making it. "I want to bring a vacuum in here tomorrow and do some more dusting in this room."

"That's a good idea, Fran. As soon as I talk to Brett about our schedule, I'll let you know what the best time would be."

"Good. Things are looking up around here."

Before Taylor could respond, Brett flung open the door of the bathroom and staggered out. Her gait was uneven, and she struggled to stay upright until she reached the now spotless table and leaned heavily against it. The look on her face was one of rage, shame, and frustration. Added to the alcohol she had consumed, she had a headache that would fell a tree, and she just wanted to crawl into bed.

"Brett, sit down, and Helen will bring you some hot soup for an early dinner. Then you and I are going to discuss our schedule."

Brett's eyes were at half-mast, her face pasty white, and she was ready to fall flat on her face. "I, I don't think I can eat anything. Please could you just leave me alone today? We can discuss the schedule tomorrow."

Brett knew she would feel better tomorrow when she got some more Scotch into her system. A steady dose of alcohol made life manageable. She'd been drinking every day for almost a year.

Taylor didn't miss the sweat that beaded up on Brett's face or the swaying of her body. "Honey, come on and let's get you into bed for now. Helen, could you bring a bowl of soup in here?"

Brett was too tired and too drunk to do anything but let Taylor lead her to the fresh bed. Clean sheets. Brett couldn't remember the last time she'd taken a shower and climbed into a clean bed. She meekly allowed Taylor to cover her up and plump up her pillow so she was sitting up. She hadn't even noticed that Fran and Helen left the room. Taylor's voice was the only thing that Brett was listening to. She had gone to sleep many a night with the memories of Taylor's sexy voice in her head.

"Taylor, here you go. Its chicken noodle with vegetables, Brett's favorite." Helen placed a tray on top of the table next to Brett's bed. Taylor pulled a chair over next to the bed and placed a towel over Brett's lap.

Brett turned, and her eyes were clouded with pain as she watched Taylor's every move. She didn't say a word, as Helen left the two women alone, closing the door behind her. Taylor slowly began to feed Brett while they stared at one another but remained silent. Taylor wanted so badly to slip her arms around Brett and tell her everything would be okay, but it wouldn't be. Brett wanted more than anything to quench the small ember of hope that was igniting in her heart. She couldn't stop her feelings for Taylor anymore than she could stop breathing. It had always been that way with Taylor. She had loved her from the very first moment she had looked into her blue eyes. Brett had been committed to her from that first evening, but fate and her own actions had been her downfall. Lack of trust had destroyed the only relationship Brett had ever wanted. Now, Taylor was sitting within inches of her, and Brett felt she was no longer worth being with for so many reasons.

Taylor tried to keep her heart from pounding as she slowly fed Brett, her hand trembling around the spoon. She had never stopped loving the woman who looked up at her with such vulnerable eyes. It would take all of her skills as a therapist to help Brett regain her physical strength, but it would take a miracle to heal her badly wounded heart.

It took Brett almost thirty minutes to finish her soup and by that time Brett's eyes were again at half-mast, as she struggled to stay awake.

"Honey, I want you to close your eyes and get some sleep. You look exhausted. We'll talk tomorrow after you get up."

"You're going to stay?"

"Yes, and I'm going to stay for as long as it takes."

"Why?"

"Because you need me, and I need to be here."

Brett didn't say another word as she slid into sleep. Her last view was of Taylor sitting next to her bed. Taylor stayed until she knew Brett was out and then bent over and placed a gentle kiss on her cheek.

"You're going to be okay, honey. I'm not going to let you be anything but okay." Taylor picked up the tray of empty dishes, turned out the light and quietly left Brett's room.

"Is she asleep?" Helen inquired as Taylor placed the tray on the kitchen counter.

"Yes, she's exhausted and has a lot of alcohol in her system. She needs to sleep it off."

"I'm so glad you're here for Brett."

"So am I Helen. She needs us to help her heal."

"Just tell me what to do."

"I'll keep you advised every step of the way. Now, if you don't mind, I think I'm going to call it an early night."

"You go right ahead. I'll take care of this. Do you want a cup of tea to take with you?"

"No thanks. Goodnight Helen."

"Goodnight Taylor." Helen watched as Taylor wearily climbed the stairs to her bedroom. Then she turned and quickly washed the dishes and put them away. Finally, she gratefully headed for her own rooms and a good night's sleep. She was certainly glad that Taylor had arrived. No one had to tell Helen that Taylor loved Brett. Seeing Taylor gently feed Brett was all that Helen needed to see.

CHAPTER 8

▼

"I'm going to kill her!" Taylor fumed, as she flew down the stairs heading towards Brett's room. She didn't announce herself but simply ripped the door open and strode into the room. Brett was sitting in a recliner, and a young woman was hanging over her, glasses in both their hands.

The young woman was a playmate of Brett's who had showed up with two bottles of Scotch. Helen had tattled to Taylor who was livid. It was only nine o'clock in the morning!

"Brett, tell your friend to leave," Taylor demanded, her voice strident.

Brett looked up at Taylor with a lazy smile while her visitor snuggled up to her. Brett wouldn't let Taylor know that she had never done anything more than drink with this woman. "She just arrived," responded Brett, a petulant whine in her voice.

"She's also just leaving and taking the alcohol with her."

Taylor was furious as she grabbed the woman's arm with one hand and the two bottles of Scotch with the other. In one continuous motion, she moved with her out of the room.

"Hey, let me go!"

"Shut up! Shame on you! If you cared about Brett you wouldn't be bringing her alcohol and drinking with her at nine in the morning or any other hour, for that matter!" Taylor was relieved to see Fran holding the front door open. "Get out of here! I don't want to see your face again as long as I'm here!"

Fran and Helen chortled with laughter as Taylor shoved the startled young woman toward her car. Taylor was a good two sizes smaller than the unwelcome guest, but at that moment she was a giant. Taylor tossed the Scotch bottles onto the passenger's seat and, as the woman's car shot down the driveway, Taylor whirled back toward the front door. She wasn't quite finished cleaning house.

She flew by Fran and Helen and startled Brett, who was sitting quietly in her chair looking out of the window. She had awakened with the draperies open for the first time in a couple of years. She hadn't yet touched the glass of Scotch that sat next to her hand. She was just sitting and enjoying the fact that she was clean and almost sober for the first time in many months.

"As long as I'm here you will not destroy yourself with alcohol or drugs! I'm not going to watch you waste away to nothing. If you don't care about yourself, think of your mother. She wants to spend her remaining time with a daughter who's sober!" Taylor hissed, snatching the full glass off the table.

This was the second time Brett had witnessed Taylor's temper, and she found it fascinating. Her blue eyes were snapping and her face was flushed. She was so beautiful. "I haven't had anything to drink this morning."

"I, I, okay, um, that's good." Taylor couldn't help but notice the glass was still full.

Brett smiled up at Taylor, surprised that Taylor would believe her. "So I think I remember you saying you wanted to work on a schedule?"

"Yes, is now a good time?"

"Sure, I have a heavy schedule, so now would be good." Brett's teasing caught Taylor off guard.

Taylor sat down on a chair next to Brett. "I thought this week that I could assess where you are with your therapy, what you can and can't do, and then we can make a plan. I'll need your permission to talk to all of your doctors in order to find out what restrictions you might have."

Brett remained silent as Taylor spoke. She could have sat there for hours, just watching Taylor talk. She was flooded with memories of the time they had been together. Every moment was etched vividly in Brett's mind. Even though her body craved the alcohol that kept her sane, she still felt the pull of Taylor deep in her heart. Anyway, now that she was unworthy of anyone's love, she could only dream.

"Brett, Brett, are you listening to me?"

"Yes, you want my permission to speak with my doctors," Brett responded, turning away from Taylor so she wouldn't see the tears in her eyes.

Taylor looked at Brett carefully. "Brett, I need you to be an active participant in your therapy. It's important that you believe in me and my abilities."

"I do believe in you." And Brett did. She had always had complete faith in Taylor. She didn't blame Taylor for refusing to believe she hadn't slept with other women. Brett had created her own reputation with just that type of behavior, but she had prayed that Taylor could see through all of the superficial layers to the real Brett. It made Brett angry to realize that it was too late for anyone, especially Taylor, to help her.

"Brett, I need to know what you're taking for medication and how much alcohol you've been drinking."

"I take Percocet for pain when I need it and a muscle relaxer when I start getting muscle cramps, and I drink about a half a bottle of Scotch a day just for fun," Brett responded, already thinking about the bottle she had stashed in her armoire. At first she had been careful to hide her alcohol from her mother. Now, she really didn't hide it from anyone. What would it matter that she was drinking herself to death? What did she have to live for? Her mother was being consumed by cancer and she had destroyed her body. She really had nothing at all to make her want to go on.

Taylor waited for Brett to continue. She was surprised that Brett was being so open. "I've been drinking every day for over two years. I've made it one of my many talents," she replied with a small bow.

Taylor winced at the self-deprecating humor. She reached out and placed her hand on Brett's arm in a comforting gesture. "I'm going to call your doctor to get some help to deal with your drinking. You're going to go through some serious withdrawal."

Brett was startled by Taylor's touch. Her hand felt hot against her skin. "I know."

"I'll be with you every step of the way."

Brett looked up into blue eyes that promised so much, and she lost her heart again to the woman who had haunted her for so many years. But she knew in her heart that she couldn't stop drinking for anyone. It was far too late. "Thank you."

CHAPTER 9

▼

By the end of the day Brett had consumed almost half a bottle of Scotch before Taylor found her lying on the floor of her room in a complete stupor. Panicked, Taylor called Brett's family doctor who arrived within an hour.

"She has serious alcohol poisoning along with so many drugs in her system. If I didn't know better, I might think Brett might have been trying to kill herself." The older doctor spoke seriously to Taylor and Brett's mother. Taylor had called Mrs. Camden immediately after calling the doctor, and she had arrived twenty minutes later.

"Oh God! I was afraid of this," Roselin cried as she heard the words that she had been dreading for almost a year. Roselin suspected her daughter was suicidal.

"I pushed her too hard." Taylor's voice was full of shame. "She didn't want me here and I pushed her."

"It's not you, Taylor. Brett has been on this path for over a year." Roselin reached out and clasped Taylor's hand. "What can we do, doctor?"

"I suggest we put her in a clinic where she can get help and get all the alcohol and drugs out of her system."

"Is she conscious?"

"Barely."

"The two women followed the doctor into Brett's room. Brett lay quietly in her bed, an IV taped to her arm. Her face was pale, her eyes sunken as she watched them approach.

"Brett, the doctor is suggesting that you go to a clinic for some help getting the alcohol and drugs out of your system."

"No!"

"But, Brett …"

"Mother, I know you just want to help me, but I won't go."

"Honey, I need you to try and get better."

"Why, Mother? What's the point?"

"You're a young woman with a long life ahead of you."

"Yeah, with this ruined body!"

Taylor had heard enough. "Your body isn't ruined! It's your attitude that's causing the biggest problems. The Brett I knew would fight to get back on her feet."

"That Brett died on a ski slope." Brett turned away from them.

"Honey, you promised me you would try once more for me." Roselin pleaded with her terribly wounded child, knowing she wouldn't be able to deny her.

Brett turned to look at her mother, naked anguish on her face. She loved her, and no one else in the world could exact promises from her. She sighed and then spoke with resignation. "I will try once more for you."

Taylor released her breath slowly as she fought to keep silent. She knew this was Brett's last chance to heal her wounded soul. She had to get through to her. Somehow she had to make Brett realize her own value.

Brett kept her word to her mother. She stopped drinking from that moment on, and within the next four hours there was no question that Brett was going through severe alcohol withdrawal. Taylor spoke to both of Brett's primary doctors, and they sent a nurse to help Taylor through the difficult withdrawal period. The nurse showed up early that next morning. Both doctors had encouraged Taylor to admit her to a hospital or specialized care center, but Taylor knew she would lose Brett completely if she forced her into that kind of facility. Taylor would make sure she received the necessary support while remaining at home. The nurse had put her on an IV to replenish fluids and to give her some respite from the stomach cramping and nausea that had started within twenty-four hours of her last drink. Mrs. Camden arrived by mid-afternoon to check on Brett, and Taylor explained clearly what to expect. The tears in Roselin's eyes pierced Taylor's empathetic heart.

"I'm sorry, Roselin."

"No, it's okay. Can I go in and see her for a minute?"

"Yes, but let me will warn you, she looks awful and feels even worse." It killed Taylor to watch Brett struggle with the pain. What was even worse was that Brett completely ignored Taylor.

"But she's cooperating?"

"Roselin, she's not even complaining, though I know she's hurting. She promised she'd trust us." Taylor gently hugged the tiny woman who cared so much for her wounded daughter. "Go sit with her."

Taylor watched as Roselin entered her daughter's room and then turned back to the nurse who was temporarily living in. "Jane is your room okay?"

"Its fine, Taylor. Thank you. Do you want me to take the night shift?"

"No, I'll stay up with Brett. You get a good night's sleep tonight. I expect tomorrow is going to be even worse."

Jane Bradford placed her hand on Taylor's arm as she spoke. "She's going to get very bad. Are you sure you want to stay here? I could get another nurse to help out."

"No, thanks very much. If Brett can do this, so can I." And Taylor meant it. She would not abandon Brett, no matter what it took. Even if Brett ended up hating her, she would not leave her without trying everything in her power to help Brett heal.

An hour later Brett began to have dry heaves and the shakes and she asked her mother to leave. Roselin wanted to stay, but Taylor convinced her to come back in a day or so when Brett was feeling a little better. She wanted Brett to have as much privacy as possible as she went through this hell and Roselin didn't need to witness her daughter's pain while in her own fragile condition.

Taylor entered Brett's darkened room and walked quietly up to the bed. Brett lay silent under the covers, her lids closed and her long eyelashes against her cheeks. Taylor sat down next to Brett hoping she would continue to sleep, but Brett's eyes flickered open and she watched Taylor.

"Honey, how are you doing?"

"Okay. It's manageable." Brett's voice was raspy from vomiting, and her skin felt clammy.

Taylor reached out and clasped Brett's hand in her own, a show of support and comfort. Too exhausted to hide her real feelings, Brett laced her fingers with Taylor's and her eyes slid shut again but not before she whispered, "I'm glad you're here."

"So am I, honey, so am I." Taylor's heart filled with emotion for the woman who was fighting so hard to heal herself.

Taylor sat quietly by Brett's side for over an hour before Brett again experienced stomach cramping followed by more vomiting.

"Get the nurse. I don't want you here!" Brett gasped, as Taylor held a bowl for her to vomit into.

"I'm not leaving you." Taylor brushed the tangled hair out of Brett's eyes. "I'm going to get a warm wash cloth for your face."

Taylor came back and gently cleaned Brett's face. She was once more lying quietly in the bed. "Taylor why did you come here?"

"Your mother asked me to, and I told you I care about you. I want to be here."

"What if I don't want you to see me like this?"

"Oh Brett, no matter what was happening with you, I'd want to be here."

Brett's hand grew slack, as exhaustion started to overtake her, and she made a slow slide into sleep. Vulnerable and overwhelmed, Brett spoke from deep in her heart. "I love...."

Taylor smiled and responded. "I love you, too." But Brett had missed her declaration as exhaustion and pain took their toll on her weary body and she slept. Taylor got as comfortable as possible on her chair and watched over the sleeping woman, her fingers still holding onto Brett's.

Brett grew steadily worse throughout the night, as dry heaves and convulsions kept her restless and shuddering in agony. She sweated until she had soaked her bed sheets. Taylor changed them around three in the morning, rolling Brett from side to side until she was lying on a dry sheet. She shivered and shook, her teeth rattling.

"I'm so cold."

"I know, honey. I put on extra blanket on your bed." Brett moaned, and her body trembled from head to toe. It was hard for Taylor to sit calmly next to her while she was in so much discomfort.

Brett cried out softly in her pain, and Taylor could stand it no longer. Standing up, she stripped her shirt and jeans off and slid under the covers, moving Brett over in the bed. Wrapping her arms around Brett, she pulled her against her own warm body trying to share her body heat with Brett. Brett rolled over and tucked her head under Taylor's chin, her arm around her waist. She mumbled against Taylor's neck.

"Go to sleep, honey."

"I remembered how you smell. You smell so good. For months I would remember your scent at the oddest times. I missed you so much. It killed me when you stopped wanting to be with me."

Brett's lips slid against Taylor's neck and, despite the circumstances, Taylor felt heat well up through her body. She could no more control her reactions than her ragged breathing. One look at Brett wounded and suffering had locked Taylor's feelings deep within her heart. She loved Brett with every fiber of her body. Taylor's presence seemed to help Brett relax, and she slept heavily tucked against

Taylor's body, her face close to Taylor's neck. Both women slept quietly until after seven the next morning. Brett was the first to awaken when she became aware of a warm body next to hers. Her eyes opened wide at the sight of Taylor's face within inches of her own. Brett allowed herself time to gaze with pleasure at Taylor's face relaxed in sleep. She was so beautiful that it made Brett ache with need and want for something she had lost years earlier. Now she knew she was less than nothing, barely able to walk. She stared at Taylor for a long time, just enjoying the feel of lying next to her. It would do no good to wish for things she couldn't have. That's what had driven her to drinking herself into a stupor in the first place. She pledged that she would do the best she could do with her therapy—for her mother, for Taylor, and for herself. She needed to find herself again.

Taylor stirred in her arms, her eyes slowly opening to find Brett watching her sleep. "How are you feeling, honey?"

"Better, not so badly right now."

"I'm glad. I'd better get up." Taylor gently pulled away from Brett and stood up next to the bed, blushing as she stepped into her pants and shirt. Brett's eyes never left Taylor. Her slender body was exactly what Brett had fantasized about long after they had stopped seeing each other. "I'll grab a shower and see if I can find you something to eat. You need to get some food into your belly."

"I don't know about that. I'm not sure if I can keep anything down yet."

Taylor smiled down at the calm, quiet woman who looked up at her with such complete trust in her eyes. "We'll start with some toast."

"Can I take a shower?"

"Absolutely. Let's tape over your IV so that you don't get it wet. Let me help you to the bathroom. You might still be a little unsteady."

Brett hated that she needed help, but she didn't complain as Taylor slowly walked her toward the bathroom. "Do you need me to help you in the shower?"

"No, I can manage. Thanks."

"Okay, honey, I'll be back in a little bit."

Brett sighed as Taylor left the bathroom. She wasn't sure what she would do when Taylor finally left for good, but she couldn't think about that at the moment. She was going to enjoy every minute she had with her. She moaned as she moved into the shower. Her body ached as she started the spray, but she knew she could do it. She had made promises to her mother and Taylor, and she renewed her vow to keep them.

CHAPTER 10

▼

For over three days Brett struggled with recurring sweats and shakes as the alcohol slowly moved out of her system. Every night, long after Brett went to bed, Taylor sat watch over her sleeping form before heading off to her own room. Jane kept watch over Brett in the daytime. Brett was drained and listless from the hammering her body had taken, but she was finally able to eat and keep the food down. Taylor had Helen make more of the vegetable soup that she knew Brett liked, and they were both sitting at the kitchen table eating while Fran cleaned Brett's room.

Taylor had convinced Brett that dressing and getting out of her room would be good for her. They were going to sit out on the deck with Brett's mother later that afternoon and soak in some sunshine. It would be the first time in a long while that Brett actually got out of the house.

The nurse had left that morning announcing that Brett was over the worst of her withdrawal from alcohol. She did make a point to Brett that if she tried drinking again, she would be right back where she started. Brett had listened half-heartedly, not able to think beyond that day. Her world had shrunk to living from moment to moment, getting by the best she could.

"So I thought tomorrow we could start with some light leg exercises. It might get your mind off of your stomach." Taylor grinned at Brett, as Brett moaned in anticipation of more pain.

"You're trying to kill me, aren't you?" Brett grinned back as she ate her soup. For the first time in a long time Brett was actually enjoying her food. She couldn't remember the last time she sat down for a regular meal.

"No, just making you suffer," Taylor chuckled. "Seriously, I won't ask you to do anything you can't do, but I need you to trust me. I've spoken to both of your doctors and they agree that you're up to full therapy."

Brett listened to Taylor and hesitated before responding. She needed to make Taylor understand clearly what Brett already knew. "Taylor, you saw my records and you spoke to the doctors. I'll never be able to ski again. Hell, I'll be lucky if I can walk without help. My left arm is almost useless. And I know I'm this way as a result of my own actions, no one else's."

"Brett, it doesn't matter how it happened, and yes, I know how extensive your injuries are. But I've worked with others who have had total knee replacement, and I know you can fully recover. Some of my clients have been able to go back to running, skiing, and almost every other activity."

"Taylor, I got drunk and skied into a tree. I deserve what happened to me!" Brett lashed out.

"Brett, honey, look at me, please. I know this isn't fair and no one, no matter what, deserves what happened to you." Taylor's face was full of compassion for Brett. She understood the anger she had just witnessed, and she wanted to channel it into helping Brett recover.

"I made a stupid decision."

"You may not have used good judgment, but we'll make sure that you recover. I promise you, I'll do everything in my power to help you, but it will take a lot of work on your part, too. I need you to believe in yourself. That same drive that made you a world-class skier is what will help you recover now."

"You don't know what it was like laying in the hospital for all those months. I almost wish I had died," Brett whispered, her head turned away from Taylor in an attempt to keep from crying.

Taylor gasped and reached out to cup Brett's chin, forcing her to look back at her. "Honey, I know exactly what you're going through. When I was fourteen, my parents were killed in a car accident and my back was broken. I also suffered internal injuries that took a long time to heal. They removed my spleen, and my kidneys were damaged. Along with that I had a fractured tibia and a concussion that caused double vision and nausea for weeks. It was months before I got out of the hospital and over a year before I could walk or move normally. I felt exactly the same way—I wanted to die."

Brett's kind heart filled with anguish for Taylor. "God, I'm sorry."

"It's okay, I fully recovered with the help of a lot of doctors, nurses, and months of physical therapy. But I want you to remember that when I ask you to work harder, I know what I'm talking about. I wouldn't ask you to do anything that I wouldn't do myself. There are times when you'll hate me and want to give up. I'm asking you now to trust me and believe in yourself. I believe in you completely."

"Why?"

"Because I know you, Brett. And your mother has faith in you as well."

"She's my best friend." Brett's eyes were bright with unshed tears.

"Your mother?"

"Yes." Brett's voice broke as she talked. "When my father died, we became even closer. She never yelled at me, no matter how badly I behaved. I've given her so many reasons for giving up on me and she never did."

"She loves you."

"And I love her. Even when I came out, she never once questioned my lifestyle. She always told me she was proud of me and knew that when I found what I was looking for I would settle down. I've disappointed her over and over. I wanted to win a gold medal at the Olympics and give it to her." Brett's eyes overflowed with tears.

"She would have liked that." Taylor grasped Brett's hand in her own as she listened. Her heart ached over the broken dreams and painful future facing Brett and her mother.

"Now, I have nothing left to offer her, and she's dying."

"You have your life, Brett. All your mother wants for you is a happy life. I'm so sorry that you're losing her, but I know she wants only for you to be healthy and happy again."

"And how can I do that?" Bitterness made her voice rough.

"You can work your ass off to get yourself in shape and start living your life again. Prove to your mother that you are the daughter she has such faith in."

"But I can't ski again."

"Maybe not, but you can coach and you will be able to walk, hike, and bike. If you work really hard you might be able to ski again. Or you can choose another profession. You're a smart woman."

"I'm a forty-two-year-old has-been skier," Brett responded, with a sardonic laugh.

"No, you're a forty-two-year-old woman who's had some setbacks."

"Setbacks! Jesus, Taylor!"

"Brett, we'll figure everything out. Let's take it one day at a time."

"'Kay, you're the boss." Brett was resigned, at the moment. She loved both Taylor and her mother and would do anything she could to justify their faith in her.

"And don't you forget it!" Taylor teased, pulling her hand away from Brett's and waggling a forefinger in her face.

For the rest of the afternoon, Taylor worked out a plan for Brett's physical therapy. Brett and her mother sat in the sunshine out on the back deck enjoying the warmth and the impressive view. It had been a long time since mother and daughter had been able to sit and just talk. Roselin couldn't remember the last time she had seen a smile on her daughter's face. Brett was also finding that her usual need to submerge herself in alcohol to keep the pain at bay was starting to disappear. She was actually looking forward to getting up in the morning.

For dinner, Helen made prepared chicken breasts, rice, and vegetables, and Brett and Roselin shared a meal for the first time in months. Taylor left them alone for most of the afternoon and evening. She knew how much they needed to spend time together right now. She came back downstairs just before Roselin got ready to leave, and the pleased look on her face when Brett hugged her mother tightly made Taylor smile. Both mother and daughter relished this time. For Roselin, it was a time to cherish and say goodbye to her only child. For Brett, these were precious moments to share and value, knowing time with her mother was growing short.

CHAPTER 11

▼

"Is that all you can say, 'Just one more'?" Brett panted as she lifted the weight attached to her left leg.

"Yep, now get going." Taylor cheerfully urged her on. True to her word, Brett had put her head down and for over a week she had faithfully followed Taylor's exercise and therapy plan. She had not had one sip of alcohol, though there were times when she craved it desperately. Her body ached, and her knees kept her awake every night, the pain undiminished by the medication she took. She cried herself to sleep every single night.

"You are mean. You know that."

Taylor laughed and continued to spot Brett. They were working out together twice a day, and Taylor was enjoying every moment of her time with Brett. They talked about Brett's years of skiing and Taylor's business. They argued about politics and laughed over bad movies they'd seen and good books they'd read. It was a time of sharing and getting reacquainted. Neither woman was wholly conscious of the bonds being formed but, as Brett stretched and strengthened her arms and legs, they were learning to trust each other and enjoy each other's company. They were becoming friends again, and that meant everything to Taylor.

"When you finish exercising, we're going for a hike. Helen made a lunch for us to take along," Taylor announced with a big grin. She expected Brett to complain.

"I can't go on a hike." Brett looked at Taylor in disbelief.

"Of course you can. I have some walking sticks for you to use to help you keep your balance."

"A hike?" Brett's eyebrows rose up under her bangs.

"Yep, and then I'm taking you to get your hair cut. You need a trim."

"A haircut! Why can't someone come here to do it?"

"Because it's time you got out of the house."

"Is that part of the program?" Brett looked at her skeptically. She recognized a ploy when she saw it.

"Yep, and you're going to have fun."

"Is that an order?"

"Yes, it is. Now come on, just one more."

Brett snorted as she huffed out ten more reps before coming to a stop, breathing heavily.

"Okay, go take a shower and meet me on the back deck in thirty minutes."

"Yes, boss."

Taylor sailed out of the room, her red hair flowing behind her. Brett's eyes stayed on her back until she disappeared. It was getting harder and harder for Brett to be around Taylor and not act upon the attraction she felt bubbling through her body. She struggled to her feet and headed for the bathroom. It surprised her how much stronger her knees felt as she stretched and prepared to shower. Brett had to admit she was feeling a whole lot better.

She scrubbed off quickly and then climbed into a pair of jeans. They hung on her slender frame, but she assumed hiking would require jeans and this was the only pair that came close to being suitable. Thirty minutes later, Brett was standing on the back porch waiting for Taylor. The view of the mountains was breathtaking, and Brett missed being on the mountain especially during the winter. She hadn't been up on the slopes since her accident. Up until that time, being in the mountains had been the main source of her happiness.

"Ready?"

Brett turned around and her breath froze in her chest. Taylor looked so damned beautiful that she could only stare. Brett had seen Taylor in just about every kind of outfit and, at one time, completely naked. That image was forever burned into her mind. But it was the casual look of a pair of faded jeans and tee shirt that Brett liked the best. Taylor had two walking sticks in her hands and a heavy pack on her back. Her smile was breathtaking, her pale blue eyes full of delight.

Unknown to Brett, Taylor's reaction was equally as overwhelming when she saw Brett wearing a pair of jeans and a sweatshirt. She looked so much like the woman that Taylor had spent the day at the zoo with. She missed that woman so very much.

"Yes, boss," Brett responded, with a grin of her own.

"Here you go." Taylor handed the walking sticks to Brett and then trotted down the back deck stairs heading for the foothills at the base of the mountains. Brett had to hurry to keep up with her, but she wasn't about to ask her to slow down and she certainly wasn't going to complain.

For over an hour Brett followed Taylor along the well-traveled hiking paths. The trees had new shoots and buds during this earliest part of spring, and everywhere were signs that the earth was renewing itself. Wild flowers and new baby animals would soon be seen along the twisting trail. Brett had grown up hiking in the mountains and started to remember how much she missed being outdoors. She was quickly becoming exhausted, her legs trembling from exertion, when Taylor came to a stop.

"I think we should stop here for lunch."

Brett just nodded her head as she immediately took a seat on a downed log in a clearing in the trees.

"How are you doing, Brett?"

"Fine."

"Brett, how are you *really* doing?" Taylor patiently waited for her to look up at her.

"I feel like my legs are going to fall off," Brett admitted with a groan, trying to keep her legs from cramping up.

"You haven't used them like this for quite awhile. You're doing very well, honey." Taylor kneeled next to Brett, pulling her pack off and rummaging through its contents. "Here, drink this while I get Helen's lunch out."

Brett took the offered bottle of juice, noticing that it was her favorite lemonade and secretly thanked Helen for her thoughtfulness.

"Here's a chicken sandwich, and we have some orange wedges."

"What no chips?" Brett's face was set in a perfect pout, which drew a grin from Taylor.

"Nope, sorry, no chips," Taylor chuckled. She knew potato chips were a favorite of Brett's.

"Ah, come on. You're being so mean," Brett teased as she took a big bite out of her sandwich. She couldn't remember the last time she had been this hungry or this exhausted. She almost felt good as she stretched her legs out in front of her and felt the warm sun begin to ease some of their tightness. Taking a big deep breath, she drew the spring freshness into her lungs. It felt really good.

"That's my job, to be as mean as possible," Taylor quipped as she sat down next to Brett and took a bite of her own sandwich. "Boy, Helen is one great cook. I don't know how you keep so slim with her cooking."

The remark was not meant to be critical of Brett and she knew that, but her response was full of bitterness. "Alcohol doesn't make you very hungry."

"Honey, I'm sorry. I didn't mean to hurt your feelings."

"Let's be honest. I'm an alcoholic."

Taylor didn't respond, she just reached out and touched Brett's face in a gentle caress, her eyes soft with compassion. It was all Brett could do to keep from kissing Taylor. She wanted so very badly to touch Taylor that, sitting so close to her, even her skin ached. "I have to take responsibility for myself, starting with my drinking." Brett turned away from Taylor before she started to cry. She knew Taylor wasn't available to her but it didn't make her want her any less.

"Honey, you're going to be okay. I know you can do this."

"Taylor, be honest with me. I'll never fully recover from my injuries, will I?"

Taylor reached out and turned Brett's face until she was looking directly at her. "I won't lie to you, ever. You have a long recovery period ahead of you, but I firmly believe you will be able to do almost anything you want. You won't be able to ski like before, and I'm sorry for that. But you have a long life to look forward to, and I know you. You'll be okay."

Brett watched Taylor's expressive face. God, she loved that face so much. "Why do you believe in me?"

Taylor was caught completely off guard by the question. She couldn't tell Brett she was still in love with her. Brett had moved on and what she was feeling for Taylor right now was gratitude. She couldn't afford to have her heart broken again. It would be too painful. But she would help Brett heal and love her silently until she had to leave. "Because I know what kind of drive it took for you to be a world-class skier. That drive is a part of you, and we just need to re-channel that energy into your rehabilitation."

"That's asking an awful lot," Brett responded, her eyes wide with doubt.

"Yes, it is," Taylor admitted, as she went back to eating her sandwich.

The two women sat for over thirty minutes while they finished their lunch and enjoyed the spectacular view. There was no need to talk. They absorbed the quiet beauty around them, and Brett let go of some of her deep-seated anger. She had missed the mountains, having spent her childhood in them, and a part of her had grieved when she turned her back on them.

"We'd better head back to the house. You have a hair appointment at three o'clock."

"I do?"

"Yes, and then we're meeting your mother for dinner."

"We are?" Brett hadn't been out of the house for so long, she wasn't sure if she was ready to be out in public. People tended to ask too many personal questions or they just stared. Everyone in the small town of Boulder knew what Brett had done to herself. She wasn't sure she could deal with another outing so soon.

Taylor didn't have to be told that Brett was scared. She saw her every feeling on her face. "You'll be fine, honey."

They stood up as Taylor settled the nearly empty pack back on her shoulders, while Brett gathered her walking sticks and stared around her at the jagged, snow covered peaks that towered over them. "I forgot how peaceful it is up here."

"It is incredibly beautiful. I thought we could hike a couple of days a week. It's good for your legs and back."

Brett didn't respond as she started to follow Taylor down the path. Taylor didn't miss the slight smile on Brett's face, and it made her heart trip in her chest. She was beginning to heal. Slowly but surely, Brett was healing.

CHAPTER 12

▼

"I want just a little bit taken off the tops and sides. I don't want it too short." Brett nervously rambled on as they entered the hair salon.

Taylor stood next to her smiling the whole time. For two very good reasons, Brett was very uncomfortable getting her hair styled in town. One was the woman at the front desk whom Brett had known intimately for a couple of weeks of fun and games. The other reason was because coming into town required her to interact with people, something she had been avoiding for over two years.

"Hi, baby, long time no see." Rachel slid her hand up Brett's stomach as she moved against her, a sexy smile on her face. Brett snagged the hand before it drifted much higher and pushed the woman away.

"Uh, hi Rach, how are you?" Her more than amorous greeting had been unexpected and unwanted.

"Good, but I'd feel much better if we could get together some night. I've missed you." Rachel's eyes were locked onto Brett's face. Taylor felt all but invisible as she watched the woman attempting to seduce Brett in a very public way. Taylor's hackles rose, and anger made her blue eyes shoot sparks.

"I'm sorry, Rach, but I'm swamped." Brett moved further away from Rachel, but Rachel just moved with her until Brett bumped into Taylor. "Uh, Rach, cut it out, please?"

Rachel's face showed dismay and puzzlement. Brett had always been ready to party with her. They didn't take each other too seriously, and that was exactly right for both of them. And then she took a closer look at Brett. She had seen her several times since her injuries but hadn't noticed how emaciated and pale she had become. "Brett, baby, are you okay?"

"I'm fine, Rach," Brett sighed, pushing Rachel away from her so they were no longer touching.

"Call me if you want to get together." Rachel spoke softly, as she moved back behind the receptionist's desk. Brett was obviously not interested in hooking up. It was then that Rachel saw the gorgeous redhead standing behind Brett shooting daggers her way. "Oh, I'm sorry."

"I'll bet you are," Taylor muttered under her breath, as she exchanged looks with Rachel.

"Ah, hah." Rachel grinned when she noticed the look on Brett's face. Brett was in love with the redhead. She couldn't mistake the look on her friend's face. And if the anger directed her way from the redhead was any indication, she returned Brett's love. "Why don't you follow me, Brett? We'll get your hair washed."

Brett stayed a safe distance from Rachel so they couldn't touch. She didn't want Taylor to think she was still playing around with Rachel. It was really important that Brett prove to Taylor she was no longer the player she had once been. Rachel gave directions to the woman who began to wash Brett's hair and then came through the main part of the salon to find Taylor moving restlessly around the waiting area.

"Hello, my name is Rachel Moore. I'm an old friend of Brett's. Can I get you a latte, water, or anything?"

"Hello, Taylor Aronson, and no I don't need anything." The words were curt but polite. Rachel didn't need to be told that the woman didn't like her.

"Why don't you sit over here? Brett's stylist will cut her hair in that chair."

"Thanks." Taylor's voice was tight, the single word full of anger.

Rachel reached out and touched Taylor's arm gently as she spoke. "Brett and I haven't gotten together for quite awhile and it wasn't important to either one of us. How long have the two of you been together?"

"We aren't," Taylor responded, her body relaxing as she listened to the woman.

Oh, honey, you two are so together, you just don't know it yet! Aloud she asked, "How's she doing?"

The genuine concern made Taylor smile and answer her civilly. "Better, she's doing a lot better."

"Good, she's a good woman. I wish her nothing but happiness. If she needs anything, please call me. I would do anything for Brett. Here's my number." Rachel handed her a piece of paper after scrawling her telephone number on it. Taylor slid it into her pocket.

"Thank you, Rachel."

"Here have a seat. She should be done with her shampoo in a couple of minutes."

"Rachel thanks again." Taylor's anger melted away as she recognized deep concern in the woman's manner.

"You're welcome." Rachel went back to the reception desk, a big grin on her face. She really did consider Brett a friend and wanted more than anything for her to find happiness. She had been so lost for many years, never quite finding what she was looking for. Rachel was willing to bet a week's pay that she would find it with the stunning woman who was with her today.

The stylist, Marc, grinned at Brett and laughed as she sat down in his chair. "Marc, I don't want it too short, just a little off the sides and top."

"Shut up, Brett. I've been cutting your hair for almost ten years. I know how you want it. By the way, you look like hell, girl."

"Thanks a lot."

"Well, your hair looks terrible, but we can fix it. How are you? I haven't seen you in town for ages."

"Good, I'm doing fine."

"Who is that stunning woman watching you like a hawk? Her hair is amazing. Does she color it?"

"That's Taylor Aronson, and her hair is natural."

"*The* Taylor?" Marc whispered as he began to trim Brett's hair.

"Yes."

"Oh, my, now I see what you mean. Those eyes could make a person melt. So are the two of you back together?" Brett had commiserated with her hairstylist when she and Taylor had broken up. He was someone she had always been able to talk to without reservation. They had known each other for years and shared many secrets with each other.

"No. She's here to help me with my physical therapy. My mother hired her."

"Oh, honey, she's not here to help you recover. Those eyes are only on you. She's watching your every move. And I thought Rachel was going to burst into flames at the looks Taylor gave her. No, honey, she wants you." Marc whispered as he flitted around Brett's head with his scissors.

"Do you think so?" Brett perked up and glanced Taylor's way. She was watching Marc cut Brett's hair, her eyes locked on the two of them.

"Oh, honey, I know so."

"I don't think so, Marc." Brett snuck another look her way. "She doesn't trust me. Besides, look at me. I'm a broken down ex-skier."

"Honey, you're a beautiful woman with a heart of gold. Court her."

"What do you mean court her?"

"If you really want to win Taylor's heart, you need to do everything in your power to prove to her that you're committed to her and worth being with. That means you need to believe in yourself. Where is the Brett I know and love, who can do anything she puts her mind to?" Marc spoke quietly as he trimmed Brett's front bangs.

"Do you think I have a chance?" Brett sighed, her heart full of emotion.

"Oh yeah, honey, a good chance. Now, what did you do when you first met Taylor? Date her."

"What if she doesn't want to date me?"

"What if she does? And, I didn't say to tell her about it. Just do it." The flamboyant hairstylist flapped his hands in exasperation.

Brett remained silent, absorbing what Marc said. Maybe she could court Taylor. She thought long and hard about it, as Marc continued snipping away.

"Voila! Aren't you a stunning butch?" Marc announced, whipping the apron off Brett.

Brett looked in the mirror and was surprised to see herself. She looked much better than she had in a long time. "Thanks, Marc. As usual, you did a great job."

"Thanks sweetie. It's nice to have you back." Brett slowly climbed out of the chair, reaching for her wallet. "Introduce me to Taylor."

Brett paid Marc and left a tip on his counter then turned and slowly walked over to Taylor. "Taylor, this is Marc Pierce. Marc, this is Taylor Aronson, my physical therapist."

Taylor winced at the introduction. She didn't want to be known as Brett's therapist. "Hello, Marc, it's nice to meet you."

Marc shook the extended hand and smiled admiringly down at the stunning woman. "So, are you making Brett work hard?"

"I'm beating her routinely," Taylor responded with a grin that transformed her face.

"Good to hear," Marc laughed, hugging Brett affectionately. "Brett, don't be a stranger."

"I won't. Thanks, Marc."

"You're welcome. It's nice to meet you Taylor." Marc congratulated himself for convincing Brett to court her. Those two women were hooked on each other. And Marc was a pure romantic. He couldn't resist a happy ending.

Brett and Taylor moved toward the reception area, and Brett began to fret. She didn't want to deal with Rachel again, but to her surprise, Rachel only waved at them and stayed behind the desk. "Nice seeing you, Brett."

Brett sighed in relief as she followed Taylor out of the hair salon. She was embarrassed that Taylor had met Rachel. It would only remind Taylor of everything she didn't like about Brett. Taylor turned and saw the look on Brett's face but wisely didn't comment as they walked slowly down the sidewalk. They were meeting Brett's mother at the restaurant in fifteen minutes. As they moved past the local stores in the center of town, people nodded their heads or called out in greeting to Brett. The sidewalks weren't at all crowded and they could stroll along next to each other with ease. They passed a Western clothing store situated next door to a women's dress shop. The Boulder Theatre was next to that. Boulder had a small town feel to it even though it was a good-sized city.

"Hi Brett."

"Nice to see you, Brett."

"Good to see you in town, Brett."

Person after person spoke to her as she and Taylor made the two-block walk to the restaurant. Brett had been a home-town favorite for years due to her incredible skiing. They had watched her compete and break record after record on the World Cup Circuit. They had also grieved when she had been terribly injured. She was one of Boulder's own celebrities, and they were very loyal. Brett stumbled once and Taylor surreptitiously reached out and supported her, leaving her hand on her arm. This helped Brett to relax and not tighten up. She was amazed that no one commented on her injuries or asked her about them. They treated her as if she was normal, and that meant everything to Brett. She had hidden herself away from the public eye for such a long time.

"Are you okay?" Taylor whispered under her breath as they approached the Mainstream Restaurant.

"Yes." Brett turned and smiled at Taylor.

Taylor's body filled with warmth as she saw Brett's face light up with a genuine smile. She couldn't stop herself from loving Brett. She was trying so hard to do everything that Taylor asked of her, including eating healthy foods, without complaint. Yes, she teased Taylor, and Taylor returned the good-natured ribbing, but up to this point, Brett had not put up any serious resistance. She had followed through with her promise and was doing everything she could to get better.

"You've had a fairly busy day."

"I'll pay for it later," Brett laughed as they entered the restaurant side by side.

Roselin watched the two women as they came in together and smiled. Anyone looking at them would assume they were a couple. Taylor's hand was resting on Brett's arm, and they leaned close to one another while they talked. Their eyes were locked on each other and obvious emotion radiated between them. Roselin sighed, and her heart settled in her chest. She had done the right thing by bringing Taylor to Boulder. Now, time and proximity would do the rest. Roselin's only goal in life was to see her daughter find happiness, and that happiness meant Taylor. She felt validated as she gazed at the two women who approached her table.

"Hi, Mother. You're looking very nice today." Brett leaned down and placed a gentle kiss on her mother's pale cheek.

Patting her daughter's back, Roselin felt tears fill her eyes as she took in her daughter's freshly styled hair and glowing skin. She was still way too slender, but at least she wasn't spending her nights drinking herself into oblivion. "So are you. I like your haircut. Hello, Taylor."

"Hello, Mrs. Camden."

"Roselin."

"Roselin. How are you feeling?"

"Fine, both of you sit down and have a look at the menu."

Taylor slid into her chair and watched as Brett placed her hand over her mother's and held it while she took her seat. Taylor felt a lump form in her throat as she observed mother and daughter. They were so close and there was genuine respect on both sides. She hadn't had enough time with own mother to develop such a strong bond and she was envious of the two of them and at the same time filled with sorrow. They didn't have much time left to spend together.

"I asked the two of you to dinner because I have a favor to ask you both."

"Anything, Mother," Brett responded, smiling softly. These were the two most important women in her life. And she would do anything for either one of them.

"Brett, you know I'm the chairman of the Children's Charity here in Boulder, and we're having our annual ball in three weeks. It's the largest event of the year, and we collect more donations than at any other time from the silent auction."

"Yes, I'll send in my donation."

"That's not what I need you to do." Roselin took a big deep breath before she continued. It took all of her effort to keep from succumbing to the pain that was her constant companion.

Taylor watched her closely and didn't miss the clouded eyes or the stiff way Roselin held herself in her chair. She's in pain, Taylor realized. She doesn't want

Brett to know. If she hadn't already developed a deep respect for Taylor's mother, she did now. Roselin loved her daughter unconditionally.

"I'm no longer able to stand on my feet for hours, and I need you to be the host of the event." Roselin spoke quietly, keeping the emotion from her voice.

"Me, but ..." Taylor's hand slid softly behind Brett's back and stopped her from immediately rejecting the idea. Taylor knew Brett's mother couldn't attend the ball and deal with her excruciating pain.

"Brett, you're well-known and have helped me before with this event. You know what's required and, let's face it, you're very charming." Roselin smiled at her daughter, her eyes held a hint of mischief.

"Mother," Brett sighed as Taylor chuckled next to her, her hand unconsciously stroking Brett's back.

"Well, you are." Roselin's eyes sparkled momentarily back at her daughter. "Will you do it? I would consider it a personal honor to have you be my stand-in."

Brett glanced over at Taylor and was graced with her gentle smile. She couldn't say no to her mother. "Yes, okay, I'll do it."

"Good, you and Taylor will have to be fitted for the right evening wear, my treat." Roselin relaxed as the waiter approached the table.

"Me, I don't need to ..."

"Taylor, Brett needs an escort."

"But, I ..."

"You'll be perfect," Roselin interrupted and then turned to the waiter as Taylor sat in stunned silence. "Ralph, what are the specials tonight?"

Brett grinned at Taylor. Her mother was a master at polite manipulation, and Taylor had just been the recipient of it. Brett was certainly pleased by the outcome. Having Taylor attend the charity event with her was a dream come true. She couldn't think of anyone else she would rather have at her side.

Roselin almost laughed out loud as she saw Taylor's reaction. Taylor hadn't been aware of the artful manipulation, and Roselin had slipped it by her before she could do anything other than agree. They would make a stunning couple, Roselin would see to it.

The meal went by pleasantly, as the three visited about the weather, their hikes, the upcoming ball, and local politics. Brett's recovery and Roselin's health issues were forgotten for a brief time. They were comfortable with each other, and the food was excellent. It was after seven-thirty before they exited the restaurant and separated. Roselin was going to stop by in the morning to discuss the upcoming charity event with Brett. She hugged Brett tightly and kissed her on the cheek.

"Thanks, honey, I appreciate your doing this for me."

"You don't need to thank me," Brett whispered, clutching her mother to her.

Taylor was surprised when Roselin turned to her and hugged her as well. "She looks wonderful."

Roselin's quiet words were for Taylor's ears only and as she hugged the frail woman back, she whispered, "Yes."

They watched Roselin safely to her car before turning to make the short walk to their own car. They remained silent until they were both seated in the SUV and on their way home. Brett was still uncomfortable driving, and Taylor sat behind the wheel of Brett's high-end Lexus SUV. "She was in pain tonight," Brett remarked as she stared straight ahead, trying to keep her emotions in check.

Taylor glanced Brett's way and saw her struggle. Her face was a mask of pain and heartbreak illuminated every time a car's headlights flashed by them. Reaching across the seat, she gathered Brett's hand in her own and held on as Brett worked to compose herself.

"I'm sorry that you got roped into attending the charity ball. If you really don't want to do it, I can get you out of it."

Taylor felt this as a rejection and tried to ignore the pain that welled up inside her chest. "If you don't want me to go with you, I won't, Brett."

"No, that's not what I meant!" Brett burst out. "I want you there."

The words were out before Brett could stop them, and she held her breath waiting for Taylor's response. "Brett, I want to go with you."

"Good," Brett sighed loudly in the darkening night and relaxed back in her seat.

Yes, thought Taylor, that's very good, and she smiled in the dark, her heart daring to hope again.

CHAPTER 13

▼

Taylor was soundly asleep in her bedroom when insistent knocking penetrated her unconscious mind and awakened her. She was in her fifth week in Boulder, and Brett was showing definite signs of improvement. Her stamina had improved and her body was beginning to show signs of muscle tone. Most importantly, Brett seemed to have found her motivation because she worked tirelessly to gain her strength back.

Taylor glanced at the clock on the bedside table and groaned. It was four in the morning. She had just fallen asleep a little after three. Being around Brett all day long and most evenings was killing her. She went to bed every night aching and longing to touch her.

"Yes?"

"It's Helen, Taylor."

Helen stayed in a suite on the east side of the house and most nights would disappear into her rooms to read or watch television before going to bed. She wouldn't emerge until it was time to prepare the first meal of the day. Something was wrong, and Taylor leaped out of bed and swung open the door startling Helen.

"What's wrong?"

"It's Brett."

"Brett!" Taylor took off down the stairs with Helen trailing behind her.

"She's crying. I heard her when I got up to get a glass of water." Helen's voice was full of concern. She had reserved a special place in her heart for Brett. Now that Brett was on the road to recovery, Helen was worried about any stumbling blocks that might be thrown up along the way.

Taylor approached Brett's room. The door was closed, and she could hear the crying and moaning from within. She didn't hesitate but went straight through the door and looked around. Brett was crumpled up in her bed, curled into a fetal position as she cried softly in the dark. Taylor was by her side in an instant.

"Honey, what's wrong?"

"Cramping, my legs are cramping up," Brett gasped as tears ran down her face. "I took a muscle relaxer and some Percocet but they're not working."

"Helen, could you get some bath towels and soak them in hot water? I'm going to massage your legs, Brett. It's going to hurt when I first start, but it will help you to relax in a few minutes."

"Okay." Brett buried her face in her pillow as Taylor pulled the sheet and blankets back. Brett was wearing a tee shirt and briefs. Her legs were pulled up tight against her thighs, the muscles of her calves straining against her skin.

"Oh God," Brett cried out as Taylor started to massage her right leg, working the knots out of her calf. "Jesus."

"I'm sorry, honey," Taylor whispered as she worked on the knots. "Maybe we should put you in a hot tub and see if you can't relax a little."

"Please. I'm willing to try anything."

Helen entered the room and saw Taylor rush toward the bathroom, her eyes wild with worry. "Helen, we need to get her into a hot tub. Both of her calves are seriously knotted up."

"Here, let me start the hot water. Go help her to the bathroom."

Taylor ran back to Brett and knelt down so that her face was level with Brett's. "Come on, honey. Let me help you into the bathroom."

"I don't know if I can walk," Brett gasped, as she attempted to swing her feet around and down to the floor.

"I'll help you." Taylor placed her arm around Brett's waist and lifted her off of the bed onto her feet.

Brett groaned, and her tight calves refused to release as she hobbled to the bathroom. Helen had gotten about four inches of hot water into the bathtub and was testing it when Brett stumbled through the door, her face drawn and sweaty.

"Thanks, Helen. I'll take it from here," Taylor announced.

"Call me if you need anything else." Helen backed out of the bathroom taking the wet towels with her.

"Come on, honey, let's get you into the tub." Taylor pulled the tee shirt off over Brett's head and then holding Brett tightly, she remained steady as Brett lifted one leg and then the other into the hot water. She gasped at the heat but immediately got some relief from the cramping as she slowly slid under the water.

Taylor knelt next to the tub, reached under the water and began to massage Brett's calf muscles, first one leg and then the other. It took several minutes, but the combined heat and massage provided a good measure of relief, and Brett lay back against the slope of the bathtub with much less pain than she had been experiencing.

Taylor leaned back watching Brett's face. Brett's eyes were closed and her breath came more regularly as she experienced some relief from her cramping. Taylor was standing up when Brett reached over and clasped her hand.

"Thank you."

"You're welcome. Are you feeling better?"

Brett couldn't keep her eyes from traveling over Taylor's body. She was wearing a blue camisole and matching panties, and she looked so sexy that Brett felt her nipples harden in response, her thighs clenching. She couldn't fail to see the hard, protruding nipples of Taylor's breasts. Taylor grew nervous as Brett stared at her, her eyes dark and locked on Taylor. Taylor's tongue lightly slid across her lips as she watched Brett watch her. She knew that look, many a night she had looked up into those same eyes while they made love. She would never forget how Brett looked when she made love to her; that look was etched in her soul.

Taylor stumbled to her feet, her eyes still unable to look away from Brett's. "I'll go straighten the sheets on your bed."

Brett watched as Taylor turned and fled the bathroom, feeling the loss. Taylor had all but run from the room. Brett knew Taylor had been physically reacting to her, and she didn't understand why she looked so terrified when she turned and left the room. Could it be that seeing Brett's badly mangled body had turned her away? Brett's heart and mind grew heavy as she stared down at her scarred torso. She hated the way she looked. She hated the fact that she had done this to herself. She had destroyed her own body with one stupid decision. She had to live with the results but obviously Taylor found her body disgusting. She couldn't prevent the tears that tracked down her cheeks.

Brett lay quietly for almost twenty minutes before standing up and drying off. The water in the tub had grown cool. She didn't know if Taylor was still downstairs. She hadn't come back into the bathroom. Brett slipped her tee shirt back on and tossed her wet panties into the clothes hamper. Toweling her hair, she entered her bedroom and found Taylor sitting on the side of her bed. She'd put on a silk dressing gown, and her eyes followed Brett as she came out of the bathroom and turned the lights off. Taylor had lit the reading lamp next to the bed, and it filled the room with a soft glow that made her look even more appealing. Brett's body raged with renewed attraction as she moved closer to the bed.

Taylor stood up as Brett approached and stepped away from the bed. "How's the cramping?"

"Gone for now, thanks. The hot bath helped a lot." Brett needed to tell Taylor it was okay to be repulsed by her injuries. She found it hard to look at her own body. She understood Taylor's feelings, or at least she accepted them.

"I'll leave you, then, to get some sleep."

"Taylor …"

As she turned to leave, she felt Brett's hand lightly touch her shoulder. The gesture was Taylor's undoing. She whirled around and threw her arms around Brett's neck, burying her face against Brett's skin. "I hate it when you hurt."

The furnace that erupted when Taylor's body collided with hers stunned Brett. She was completely overwhelmed and unable to do anything except to wrap her arms around Taylor's slender back and hold her tightly. She would be content to stand there for hours if it meant she got to keep on holding Taylor.

Brett breathed in the scent she knew by heart as she buried her nose in Taylor's hair. She had missed Taylor so much for so many years. Memories flooded through her mind as her body recognized the one woman Brett had loved completely.

Taylor's lips moved of their own volition tasting the skin along Brett's neck and jaw—soft, fragrant skin that she had memorized long ago—drawing her closer and closer to Brett's wonderful lips, lips that had once kissed her into complete submission. The single thing she had loved most about Brett was that she had kissed Taylor like she was the only person in the world that mattered. Brett sucked in her breath as Taylor's mouth covered hers in a kiss that tore through her senses. Both women groaned as their mouths met and memory took over. Lips and tongues mated, and they tasted each other, intent on making up for lost time. Long, deep kisses, lips full and wet, Brett's tongue entered Taylor's mouth drawing a moan from her. Taylor felt Brett's naked thigh push between her legs and slide long and hard against Taylor's wet center. Her hips jerked at the pressure. The robe slid open, and it was Brett's wetness on her thigh that made Taylor move her hand down under the tee shirt and across Brett's backside, pulling her hips tight against Taylor's thigh. She wanted to give Brett pleasure, the feel of her almost too much to bear.

"Oh God!" Brett stumbled away from Taylor, her eyes closed as she realized how close they were to making love. "I'm sorry."

Taylor wasn't sure what to expect from Brett, but an apology wasn't it. She was hurt and she blindly turned toward the bedroom door, trying to flee to her room.

"Taylor, wait, please?" If Brett's voice hadn't trembled when she spoke, she wouldn't have turned around.

"What?" Taylor's eyes were full of pain, and Brett knew it was her fault. She hadn't meant to hurt Taylor and she needed to make her understand.

Brett stepped closer to Taylor and reached up, placing her hand softly against Taylor's face. "I want you so much and I don't know why you would want me."

Taylor jerked in surprise as she heard the self-deprecation in Brett's voice. She stepped close to Brett, wanting so badly to touch her, but she didn't. "I love you, Brett. I've always loved you."

Brett's eyes filled with tears as she absorbed the words. "You love me?"

"Very much."

"But I'm a mess. I have a deformed body and no job, and I'm an alcoholic."

Taylor's eyes signaled anger and she stepped away from Brett, furious with her. "You're not deformed, and yes, you are an alcoholic. But you're recovering. If you don't have faith in yourself, how can you expect anyone else to have any?"

Taylor started to leave Brett's room, but Brett stopped her again with a quietly spoken comment. "I have faith in you."

"Oh, Brett, I have faith in you, too."

"Don't give up on me, please?" Brett reached for Taylor's hand.

"I won't, honey." Taylor smiled. "Go back to bed and get some sleep."

"You won't leave?" Brett couldn't keep the panic from entering her voice.

"No honey, I'm not leaving," Taylor promised. Leaving was the farthest thing from Taylor's mind.

"Good."

"Goodnight," Taylor called softly. She left the room and climbed the stairs to her own bedroom, her mind in a jumble after hearing that Brett was still in love with her.

Brett crawled under the covers and laid quietly, her fingers gliding across her lips. She couldn't believe that Taylor loved her. Her body still vibrated with attraction for Taylor.

From an early age Brett had known she loved women, in particular women's bodies. By the time she graduated from college with a degree in Business Administration, she knew making love to women was something she enjoyed very much. She was fascinated by breasts and thoroughly enjoyed kissing a woman's body from head to toe. There was nothing like the taste and scent of a woman when she covered her clitoris with her mouth and drove her to an orgasm. Brett prided herself on her lovemaking. She never left a woman's bed without giving her complete pleasure. Rarely did she allow another woman to touch her, however. Somehow, not loving someone made it impossible to want another woman touching her that intimately. That's how she had known she was madly in love with Taylor. She craved her touch almost as much as she wanted to make love to Taylor, and the hunger never went away.

She had tried to bury that hunger by playing harder and drinking more after Taylor had broken up with her. It hadn't worked, and she had grown increasingly dissatisfied with casual sex of any kind. It had been over a year before her accident that she had touched another woman. And that had been part of the problem.

Juliet Hart had pursued Brett for months, wanting to tame the wild, untouchable skier. Brett lived her life wildly, yet remained aloof, detached, and some women found this very appealing. Juliet was one of those women. And Brett was not immune to Juliet's considerable charms. Juliet had been a model for several years before becoming a representative of a large public relations firm in Los Angeles. Brett met her when Juliet's firm was representing the U.S. Ski Team and planning all of their events. Juliet was petite, feminine, and a stunning blond woman who was not shy about making her feelings known. Juliet wore the most fashionable clothes, she ate at the most famous restaurants, and she drove a fire engine red Jaguar convertible. There wasn't a gay woman in Los Angeles that wouldn't find her sexy and very appealing. She was financially set due to her high salary and astute investing, and nothing was off limits to Juliet. She pursued many women, sometimes more than one at the same time, and she usually got what she wanted. She had wanted Brett and had gone after her with a vengeance. Brett had played with her, attending all-night parties and drinking oceans of champagne, but after almost two months of being pursued and hours of kissing, Brett had never touched her, and that was driving Juliet crazy. No one had put Juliet off that long. Brett would be a formidable catch, and that made her even more appealing.

After weeks of waiting, Juliet was determined to make something happen. She was the one who suggested that they go to Brett's home in Boulder. Brett rarely took women to her home. It had been off limits because of Brett's plan to share it with the one woman she would be with for the rest of her life. Brett no longer believed that would happen so she agreed to Juliet's request. Juliet had planned it all—a week of playing, during which she planned to seduce Brett. No one held Juliet off for long. And the wild and charismatic skier was like a drug to Juliet. She wanted her very much in a very physical way. Love had nothing to do with it. Brett was charming, funny, drop-dead gorgeous, and had an incredible body. Along with her fame, she was undeniably appealing, and refusing her made Juliet even more committed to seducing her.

The second night at the house in Boulder Juliet zeroed in on Brett, plying her with several glasses of Scotch after a romantic dinner for two, provided by Helen. They were lounging on the living room couch, Juliet draped over Brett, when she decided to end the drought. Reaching between their bodies, Juliet slid down the zipper on Brett's silk dress pants and placed her hand between Brett's thighs, cupping her wet center.

"Whoa, Juliet," Brett had mumbled, pulling her hand away.

"Brett, baby, let me make you come. You know you want me," Juliet had purred, her fingers reaching once more for Brett's wet center.

"Juliet, don't." Brett's words were slurred as she pushed Juliet off.

"What the hell is wrong with you?" Juliet shrieked, standing next to Brett, angry as hell.

"Nothing is wrong with me. I just don't want to fuck!" Brett snarled, getting unsteadily to her feet.

"You are a fraud! You haven't touched me in two months! The great lover! Ha, you probably can't ski either!" Juliet was livid. No one rejected her more than once.

"Just because I don't want to fuck you doesn't mean I can't ski!" Brett lashed back. "Maybe I don't want to fuck someone who's been with half of Los Angeles."

Juliet jerked back as if she'd been slapped when she heard Brett's comment.

It was no secret she slept around, but so had Brett. She was furious that Brett was judging her behavior. Brett was no better and she had no right. "Prove it!"

"Prove what?" Brett glared at the woman.

"That you can ski!"

The angry dare was more than Brett could take in her drunken state. The one thing that Brett could do better than anything was ski. They piled Brett's equipment into the car and Juliet drove them to the pass. It may have been after ten at night, but the chair lift was still running. Even though Brett had been drinking, Juliet egged her on. Finally, they both stood at the top of the downhill run. Brett had looked out over the sparkling snow and felt her body calm down. Here was where she felt most at home—on the mountain skiing. She was most completely alive when she sailed down the snow-covered slopes.

"Watch this." Those were the only words Brett said as she took off and headed down the steep slope. She executed the first half of the run flawlessly. Her natural, God-given talent and dedication to hard work were obvious as she sailed down the mountain. The raw beauty of Brett's skiing stunned Juliet as she watched Brett gliding through turn after turn. But fate was not kind that night, and too much alcohol made Brett careless. She overcorrected on a sharp turn. The minute she did, she knew she was in trouble. She crossed the ski slope out of control and slammed into a tree at full speed. She was knocked cold before she could feel the intense pain caused by her body being brutally crushed against the unforgiving trunk and low branches of the century-old Douglas fir. Thankfully she remained unconscious as she lay in a crumpled heap at the base of the tree.

Juliet screamed as she witnessed the accident from above. By the time the ski patrol had gotten to Brett, Juliet was completely hysterical, her words coming out in a jumble as she tried to explain what happened.

"It's my fault, God, it's my fault," she cried over and over as she watched them load the critically injured woman into the ambulance. At the hospital, she told the police what had happened and waited while the emergency room staff worked frantically to keep Brett alive. She stayed until Mrs. Camden arrived, and then she had left. Her guilt over the accident and her fear for Brett made her run away. She had gone back to Brett's home and packed her things and fled back to Los Angeles. She hadn't spoken to Brett since that night. Not even after Brett was released from the hospital had Juliet contacted her. It was as if they had never known each other.

Brett shuddered in her bed as she remembered waking up in the hospital, her mother sitting next to her bed.

"Mom, what …"

"Honey, you've been in a very bad skiing accident and you had to have emergency surgery."

"I'm sorry, Mother, I'm so sorry …" Brett slid back into morphine—induced sleep as her mother watched and cried for her only child. She would have to tell her the horrible news. Her career as a skier was over. Mrs. Camden knew that information was going to destroy her daughter. Since she was a young child, it had been her dream to compete and win a gold medal in the Olympics. Brett had been less than a year away from her chance to do just that, and now that dream was destroyed. Roselin was angry at the fates that put her daughter in the hospital, but she knew Brett's injuries had been brought on by her own unfortunate decision. Brett would know that when she woke up, and Roselin refused to put any more guilt on her only child while she was in this fragile condition. She was grateful that Brett was alive.

Brett closed her eyes and willed the memories away. That was in the past, and there was nothing she could do about it now. She had been stupidly careless and was now living with the results. How could she think that Taylor could love her? How could she, knowing what Brett had done to herself? But she did, and that was a miracle. Brett would do anything to regain Taylor's trust. Until she had something to offer Taylor, she wouldn't sleep with her. She would get better and she would figure out some kind of a career. She would make herself worthy of Taylor's love.

Taylor lay in bed, unable to sleep, her body still aching after being held by Brett. She had managed to keep her feelings under control until tonight. Seeing Brett so helpless and vulnerable had made giving in to her emotions so easy, and then that kiss … it was so perfect, so Brett. God, she made Taylor crazy. She wasn't irreparably damaged. She was hurt, but Taylor could help her heal. Being an alcoholic was no small problem, but Taylor knew Brett could deal with it. It was the fact that Brett didn't realize her own worth that disturbed Taylor the most. Taylor couldn't make Brett value herself—that was completely up to Brett. Taylor prayed that Brett would figure everything out, because if she didn't, they couldn't be together.

CHAPTER 14

▼

Nervously, Brett pulled on her formal dinner jacket. At her mother's request, she was wearing an elegant silk evening suit in jade green. Brett was not comfortable wearing an evening gown, but her mother had chosen her outfit well. The smartly cut designer suit fit her perfectly, and she smiled at her reflection. She was starting to feel more like the Brett she used to be. She was now doubling her workouts, against Taylor's recommendation, but Brett had a goal. She was going to try to coach the U.S. Ski Team before their next winter season. She needed to be in better physical and mental shape to do that.

Brett gathered her wallet and keys and slipped them into the front pocket of her jacket before exiting her bedroom. She was anxious to see Taylor. Since the night of their kiss a little over a week earlier, neither woman had touched the other. But attraction shimmered in the air when they were together. Brett was about ready to combust, but she had a plan. She had started by placing a vase of freshly gathered wildflowers in Taylor's room. Then she had arranged a surprise hike that she had planned, including a gourmet picnic meal. They had laughed together at two romantic comedies Brett rented for a "movies and pizza" night at home. Then Brett invited Taylor to go for a walk in the moonlight one night. Not once did Brett do anything more than quietly visit with Taylor. Taylor was becoming increasingly puzzled by Brett's behavior, but she was unwilling to take a chance by touching her again.

That evening Brett had another surprise for Taylor. A black velvet box was sitting on Taylor's dresser with a note. The note had only one line: *Thank you, Brett.* She had found a splendid pair of antique diamond earrings with a matching necklace to go with Taylor's evening gown. Brett hadn't seen the dress on

Taylor yet, but her mother had described it to her in detail. It was a pale mint green that draped low on her back and molded perfectly to her curvaceous figure. With her red hair and blue eyes, Brett knew she would be stunning.

"Brett, you look beautiful." Taylor's soft voice reached her as she came down the stairwell.

"You look ..." Brett was speechless as she watched Taylor approach her. Stunning was too tame a word.

Taylor's smile was entirely too sexy as she reached up and placed a kiss on Brett's cheek. "I found your gift on my dresser. Thank you."

"I see." Brett's eyes dropped to the diamonds nestled in Taylor's cleavage. She envied the diamonds. "Are you ready?"

"Yes." Taylor wrapped a matching silk shawl around her shoulders and linked her arm with Brett's.

Brett's heart pounded as she smiled into startling blue eyes and whispered to Taylor, her heart on her sleeve, "This is a date, you know."

Taylor's eyes crinkled up with humor. "I know," was all she said, but it was enough.

Brett almost floated out to the waiting limousine. Her mother's driver tipped his hat at the beautiful couple.

The early dinner and auction were held at the downtown Boulder City Center Ballroom. Brett's charismatic charm took over, and she made her mother proud. Her opening remarks were clever and humorous, as was her direct and heartfelt plea for donations to the children's charity. Many people approached her and not once did she fail to introduce Taylor. She kept her hand on Taylor's back, or Taylor's arm was resting on hers. There was no mistaking that the two women were there together. Brett was attentive, solicitous, and terribly cute as she wooed Taylor. It was after eleven, the dance floor was crowded with dancing couples, and everyone was having a raucously good time. Taylor asked to be excused for a moment to use the rest room. She had been balancing on her high heels for several hours and needed to slip away for a few minutes to freshen up.

"Did you see Brett? She's back to her old tricks, sleeping with every gorgeous woman she can find. Who can blame her? That redhead is a knockout."

Taylor tried to let the carelessly spoken words bounce off her as she entered the bathroom. She couldn't help overhearing the two women's conversation. They abruptly stopped talking when they saw her, but that didn't stop Taylor from calling them on their gossip.

"It's really too bad that you don't know Brett at all. She's a generous and honest lover. She would no more sleep around on a partner than I would. You should be careful what you say. Slander can be very expensive."

The two women fled the bathroom while Taylor smiled sweetly at them as she exited the bathroom stall. She saw a grinning Rachel leaning against the sink. She looked delectable in a dark navy gown, her large breasts all but overflowing the low-cut bodice. Taylor couldn't help but let her eyes linger momentarily before looking up into Rachel's laughing eyes.

"Nice dress."

"Thanks, same to you. Nice slam." Taylor raised her eyebrows as she washed her hands. She didn't know how to respond. "You were right though. Brett would never ever cheat on you. She's madly in love with you. She has been since the first night she met you."

"How do you know?"

"Because she told me. Brett and I have known each other for years. We only slept together once in awhile, and it meant nothing to either of us. We haven't slept together since before her accident."

"Why?"

"Because Brett didn't want to sleep with other women after you broke it off. You underestimated how much you hurt her."

"What do you mean?"

"Her reputation was all hype. She didn't sleep around all that much even before she met you, but afterwards, she refused to let anyone touch her. There were only a couple of women before she was injured."

"You sound like you care about Brett very much," Taylor remarked, watching Rachel carefully.

Rachel laughed softly. "Oh I do, but not in the way you're implying. Brett is the most loyal friend a person could have. She's never once refused when someone asked her for help. She came to my rescue a couple of times. I want to see her happy. You're the one woman that makes her happy. She loves you."

"I love her."

"I know you do."

"She still doesn't believe she deserves to be with me."

"Then convince her." Rachel grinned as she walked out of the bathroom with Taylor. "You're a smart girl."

Taylor flashed a quick grin Rachel's way. "Yes, I am. Thanks."

"You're welcome."

Taylor approached Brett who stood talking to a group of people about the charity for children. She was taking her hosting job very seriously and continued to solicit donations. As Taylor approached, she saw a particularly stunning brunette slide her hand around Brett's waist up under her jacket. Taylor saw red as the woman's hand started to slide familiarly over Brett's backside. Brett's hand reached back and caught the woman's hand pushing it discreetly away from her. At the same time, she turned to the woman, her eyes clear and direct as she spoke softly, just loudly enough for the woman and Taylor to hear.

"Do you mind? The only person who can touch me like that is Taylor." Brett reached behind her and gathered Taylor close to her, her arm around Taylor in a possessive grip. Taylor looked up into the brown eyes that held her captive and she moved closer, her smile for Brett alone. She couldn't have been more pleased with Brett's actions.

It was after two-thirty before their driver dropped them off at home, and by that time Brett was almost out on her feet. Her legs ached from standing all night, but nothing could tarnish her feelings. The night had been perfect. She and Taylor entered the dark house in silence, the magic of the evening still shimmering around them. The ball had been a tremendous success clearing over eight hundred thousand dollars in checks in one night for the children's charity. Brett's mother would be pleased with the results.

"Taylor," Brett stopped inside the front door and took her hand pressing it against her heart as she spoke. "I had a wonderful evening with you."

"I did too." Taylor waited and watched as Brett just stared at her.

"Can I kiss you goodnight?"

Taylor smiled at the nervous woman, moving up close to her. She needed to kiss her. "Yes."

Brett moved slowly, her hands sliding up to hold Taylor's face as she softly pressed her lips against Taylor's. Taylor whimpered as Brett's tongue drifted over her top lip before entering her mouth. Slowly Brett loved Taylor's mouth until Taylor was trembling. Taylor's fingers played in the hair at the nape of Brett's neck as her body molded to Brett's. Brett took her time kissing Taylor until she couldn't stand anymore. Then she moved gently away and held Taylor in her arms.

"I want to be with you so badly, it hurts," Brett whispered, as she looked into blue eyes full of passion.

"I want to be with you."

"Can we wait a little longer? I want to be someone you can be proud of and I'm working very hard to make that happen."

"I am proud of you, Brett."

"I need you to believe in me. You told me that. I want to get my life back and be with you for the rest of it. I'm going to work as hard as possible to get healthy. I called the head of the U.S. Ski Team, and they're interested in me as a coach. But I have a lot of work to do before that can happen. Will you help me?"

Taylor knew this was the moment of truth for her and Brett, and she didn't hesitate for a moment. "Yes, I will help you."

"Do you mind waiting a little while longer?"

"Yes I do, but I understand." Taylor grinned back at her.

"I love you, Taylor. I've always loved you."

"I love you, Brett, and I'll wait as long as it takes."

"Thank you." Brett began to cry softly. Her tears revealed to Taylor more clearly than anything else how deeply Brett loved her.

CHAPTER 15

▼

Brett and Taylor's world revolved around working out, spending time with Roselin, and reacquainting with each other. Roselin's health was slowly failing, her strength disappearing as the cancer ravaged her body. She refused to do anything other than manage the pain, which at times was excruciating. Brett finally talked her into moving into the other upstairs bedroom in her home. She didn't want her mother alone in her house. Roselin and Brett talked for hours, recognizing that time was precious, and Taylor often joined them.

Brett woke up early and went to bed late, working out religiously. Many nights she slept with ice bags or heating pads to alleviate some of the pain from overworking her body. Taylor cautioned her about working too hard, but Brett continued to press herself, never once complaining. This was the Brett that Taylor had first known. Driven and competitive, undaunted by anything that stood in her way, she was going to be the best ski coach in the world. Taylor believed in her and knew she would be successful.

"Hey, Taylor, how's Brett?"

"Good, Jeb, she's downtown doing some shopping."

"Good for her." Jeb was a man who loved a good sale.

"I just called to check in. How's business?"

"Going gangbusters, we're going to have a record quarter."

"Excellent! I'm sorry I'm not able to be of more help."

"No worries, honey, you trained your staff well. Hey, are you guys up for me to come for a quick visit? I have some business I need to review with you and I'd love to see Brett again."

"Let me check with her. Her mother is getting worse every day, and I don't want to upset her routine. I think Brett would love to see you, though, and I miss you like crazy."

"I miss you too. Why don't you talk it over with her and then get back to me?"

"Jeb, is everything okay?"

"Everything is fine. I just want to see my best friend and talk over a new idea I have."

"Okay, I'll talk to Brett tonight. She's taking me to the movies."

"Are you two doing okay?"

"We're doing fantastic, other than that we aren't sleeping together yet."

"You're kidding me!"

"I wish! She wants to wait until she has things a little more together. She's had a rough couple of months."

"How's she doing with the sobriety thing?"

"Really well. She doesn't seem to have any issues with not drinking, but then we rarely go anywhere where alcohol is the main attraction."

"Did you tell her I'm an alcoholic?"

"No, that isn't my business to tell."

"Oh, honey, you can tell her. I'm not ashamed of it."

"I know that."

"She's going to have a very tough time when she loses her mother."

"I know. Roselin is such a lovely woman. You'd really like her. She's just so gracious and honorable, and she loves Brett without reservation. Brett is so much like her."

"I'd like to meet her."

"I'll call you tomorrow, okay?"

"Good. Say hello to Brett, and tell her about me. It might help her."

"I will."

It wasn't until after Helen started preparing dinner that Brett returned home. Taylor hadn't heard from Brett since early afternoon. She had tried to reach her on her cell phone several times, but Brett was not picking up. Taylor was beginning to get vaguely uneasy.

"Taylor, sit down and eat with me. Brett probably got held up in traffic." Roselin suggested as she watched Taylor move restlessly around the living room.

Taylor tried to mask her feelings as she slid into a chair at the dining room table across from Roselin. Roselin's face showed nothing but a welcoming smile but she too was beginning to get worried about Brett.

Brett had finished her shopping hours earlier but as she was loading her packages into her SUV she ran into a couple of World Cup skiers who spent part of the year training in Boulder.

"Brett, my God, how long has it been? Where have you been, girl?"

"Hi Max, hey Lucas, how are the two of you?"

"Pumped! We are rippin' up the slopes this year. How are you, girl? We haven't seen you around forever." Max was a daredevil of a giant slalom skier who'd been on the ski circuit for years. Lucas had just started skiing the year before Brett's accident.

"I'm doing well, thanks. What's your placement this year?"

"Seventh—can you believe it? There are a few youngsters wreaking havoc with the standings, but I think this year is going to be good for me."

"I'm listed eleventh," Lucas responded with a grimace. Standings on the circuit did one of two things. They gave everyone a snapshot of how well a skier was doing, and the higher the placement in the standings, the more a skier was offered sponsorship. Sponsors paid for skiers to compete, and the more sponsors one had the more money a skier made. Brett had been rated number one for the last three years she skied and had turned away some of the lucrative contracts other skiers would have jumped through hoops to have. She didn't need the money and her only goal was to win a gold medal in the Olympics. Taking money from sponsors could be very distracting with all of their demands for time. And Brett hadn't wanted to be distracted from her goal.

Both men knew about Brett's accident. Everyone associated with skiing had heard about it and mourned for the loss of such a talent. Max's heart had broken at the thought of the charismatic skier being so badly injured.

"Brett, how's the recovery? You're looking terrific."

Brett flinched at the question. She knew that news of her accident had spread through the ski circuit like wildfire. "I'm doing well, thanks."

"Hey, come on. Let's go to the Downslope and get a drink. We'll catch you up on all the gossip"

The Downslope was a tavern known for its food and drinks and popular with the skiing set. Run by an ex-skier from the seventies, the walls were covered with pictures of world-class skiers. Brett had all but lived there while in Boulder before her accident.

"Sure." Brett thought about calling Taylor and letting her know what she was planning. She was afraid to. Shouldn't she be able to make decisions like this on her own and be trusted?

"Come on, girl, I can't wait to tell you what happened in Austria last month. You'll love it. We got crazy." Max threw his arm affectionately around Brett's shoulders as the three of them headed down the sidewalk toward the restaurant and bar.

They found seats in the crowded bar area and before Brett knew it she had a full glass of Scotch in front of her. Max and Lucas filled her in on the last couple of years on the ski circuit. She didn't take a drink from the glass, but her eyes kept glancing down and she felt the pull deep in her body. What would it hurt to have a glass of Scotch? She was getting better and could handle it. She was an adult, wasn't she?

For almost an hour the glass sat untouched in front of Brett while she laughed and visited with the two men. She missed skiing so much, and the conversation fed her need to hear about what was going on in the world she had once been so much a part of.

"Brett, drink up. It's time for another round." Lucas nudged her and tried to catch the eye of the waitress.

Brett placed her hand around the glass and imagined drinking the Scotch. Her mind was saying no, but her body was saying yes.

"Brett, is that you?" Rachel approached the table.

"Hi Rach."

"Hey Max, Lucas, how are you?"

Rachel was also a regular at the Downslope. She had partied with many of the skiers on the circuit.

"Good, Rach, grab a chair."

"I will, but I need to talk to Brett for a minute. Can you excuse us?" Rachel was shocked to see Brett in town at a bar, especially without Taylor.

Rachel tugged on Brett's arm to get her to stand up. Brett placed the drink back on the table and followed Rachel to the women's restroom.

"Brett, what are you doing here?"

"What do you mean? I can go wherever I want," Brett snarled.

"Where's Taylor?"

"She's at home." Brett hung her head when she uttered the words. She was ashamed of herself.

"Brett, honey, go home. You love Taylor and she loves you." Rachel also knew that Brett was struggling with alcohol. She wouldn't let her friend slide back into a bottle. "Did you drink?"

"No. I thought about it but I didn't drink."

"Good, go home. Everything you want is at home. Don't be an idiot and risk losing Taylor. Why would you hang out at a bar when a beautiful woman is at home waiting for you?"

Brett began to cry. "I miss skiing and being on the circuit. That was my life and now it's gone."

Rachel reached out and hugged Brett tightly. She'd lost so much. "You're going to be okay. I know you miss it but you're going to be okay. Come on let's get out of here."

Rachel pulled Brett out of the tavern and with her arm slung around her waist they headed down the sidewalk. "Where's your car parked?"

"Two blocks down Main."

"Come on."

They got within half a block before either woman saw Taylor leaning against Brett's car, her eyes focused intently on them. Worry and pain had made them glassy, her face pale. She didn't say a word. She just stood up and started to turn away from them.

"Taylor, wait! This isn't what it seems." Brett cried as she realized what Taylor was thinking. Taylor kept walking.

"Brett, stay here." Rachel took off running in order to catch up with the devastated woman. Taylor was crying as she moved quickly to Roselin's car. Seeing Brett with Rachel had shocked her. She had really believed in Brett. Rachel caught up with Taylor and grabbed her arm. "Taylor, wait."

"Let go of me!" Taylor whipped around and pulled away from Rachel.

"Not until you listen. Brett wasn't with me. I was walking her to her car. I found her in the Downslope Tavern."

"She was drinking?" Taylor's face grew white, her concern for Brett overcoming her anger.

"No, she didn't drink. She had a full glass of Scotch in front of her, but she didn't drink."

"Why?" Taylor's face was covered with tears.

"She ran into two guys she used to know when she was skiing. They were catching up on the gossip. She misses skiing, Taylor. It was her life, her dream, and now it's gone."

Taylor's respect for Rachel was renewed. "She has been working so hard. She wants to be the coach of the U.S. Ski Team."

"Good for her. She needs to stay connected to skiing." Rachel relaxed as they spoke. Taylor had stopped crying. "She didn't do anything wrong, Taylor."

"We were worried about her. She didn't call and we couldn't reach her on her cell phone."

"Then go chew her ass off for not calling you!"

Taylor grinned at Rachel. "I'm beginning to like you an awful lot."

Rachel laughed. "I like you. I like Brett with you. She loves you. Go chew on her. I'm going to leave the two of you to figure this out."

"Thanks Rachel."

Rachel shoved Taylor in the direction of Brett's car, where Brett stood watching them uneasily.

Taylor walked the half block back, her eyes locked on Brett. Brett didn't know what to say as she watched Taylor approach her. She waited to see what Taylor would do. Taylor saw raw fear on Brett's face, and her anger dissolved.

"Brett, are you okay?"

"Yes, I didn't drink. I'm sorry I was gone so long."

"You should have called to let us know you were going to be late. Your mother and I were very worried."

Brett flinched at her words. "I'm sorry. I was talking to some guys from the ski circuit. We were catching up. I miss skiing so much."

Taylor's eyes filled with tears as she listened to Brett and then she reached out and gathered her in her arms. "I know, honey."

Brett started to cry, her body shaking with sobs. "I wanted to ski in the Olympics and win a gold medal."

"I know. I'm sorry you won't be able to do that. I would do anything to give that back to you."

"I'm sorry I hurt you." Brett wrapped her arms around Taylor and buried her face against Taylor's neck. "I wouldn't hurt you for the world."

"I know, honey. It's okay—everything is going to be okay."

"I love you, Taylor, so much. I will always love you."

"I love you, Brett I'm so proud of you that you didn't have a drink. You're going to be just fine."

"Rachel called me an idiot for staying at the bar."

Taylor chuckled softly, Brett sounded so indignant. "She told me to chew your ass off for not calling me."

"Are you?"

"Am I what?"

"Going to chew my ass off?"

Taylor smiled as she tightened her hold on Brett. "I think I'll wait until you really make me mad."

"Rachel is a good friend."

"Yes, she is. Let's go home. Are you going to be okay to drive?"

Brett pulled away from Taylor and wiped her face. "Yea, I'm fine. How did you find me?"

"I drove Roselin's car and I saw your SUV parked on Main Street."

"I love you, Taylor." Brett touched Taylor's face. "I'm sorry."

"I know. Come on, honey. Let's go home."

The two women drove home and entered the quiet house together. Neither woman said a word as they stood in the living room until Taylor reached out and squeezed Brett's hand. "Go to bed, honey. We'll talk in the morning."

Brett's heart pounded loudly in her chest. "Are we okay, Taylor?"

"We're fine, Brett."

Both women headed for bed, exhausted and a little raw over what had transpired. Brett lay awake long into the night, thinking of her behavior and the impact on Taylor. She had seen the look of hurt on Taylor's face and she would give anything to take back her actions.

The following day was taken up by workouts and business details for Taylor. Brett had spent over an hour on the telephone in her office. Taylor waited to talk to Brett until after they had finished eating dinner with Roselin. She had grown quickly tired and excused herself to go to her room a short time after dinner. Taylor and Brett were attending the late movie at the Boulder Theater and finally had a chance for some conversation on the trip to town.

"Honey, Jeb and I spoke yesterday and he'd like to come up for a quick visit to talk to me about some business stuff. He'd also like to see you. Would that be okay with you?"

"Of course it would. Taylor, is your business okay? I know you're refusing my mother's payments." Brett had been bothered by that fact since she had discovered it over a week ago.

"Brett, my business is fine. Honey, I can't let your mother pay me for something I choose to do."

"But ..."

"No buts, please. Jeb also asked me to tell you something. He's a recovering alcoholic, honey, and he wanted you to know. If you need to talk with him about anything, all you have to do is call him."

"That's nice of him. You know, most of the time I don't miss drinking at all. It's kind of nice to be totally aware of everything around me. Then out of the blue I want a drink. It's so odd. Last night the glass of Scotch sat in front of me and I wanted to take a sip. And then I thought of my mother and you and it didn't seem so important to drink. Does my being an alcoholic bother you?"

"No, honey, it doesn't." Taylor slid her hand over Brett's muscled thigh. "I love you just the way you are."

"Yeah! You want to skip the movie and go to lookout point and neck?"

"I'd love to." Taylor laughed at the suggestion. Brett was always surprising her with unexpected comments like that. The night before was forgotten as the two women allowed themselves to enjoy the evening ahead of them. Taylor knew Brett's struggles were much more than alcohol. She was finding herself day by day, and each day was going to be a challenge. She understood how much Brett missed her former life.

"Here's an even better idea. We go to the movie and then I do my level best to seduce you when we get home."

"I like that idea even better." Taylor's face lit up with pleasure. She was waiting for Brett to make the first move when it came to their lovemaking. Brett reached down and covered Taylor's fingers with her own, holding her hand tightly as they drove the short distance to town. She loved Taylor with every breath in her body, and earlier that day she had told her mother she was going to marry Taylor. Her mother had given her daughter her blessing and a suggestion. Maybe she should talk to Taylor about her plans. She also had pointed out to Brett how important it was to talk to Taylor about her feelings about her accident and her injuries. She shouldn't keep anything from Taylor if she wanted to be with her.

Tonight Brett was going to do that and more. She had a single carat blue-white diamond set in a solitary setting burning a hole in her pocket. She had thought to wait until she had a job and her future was more stable, but her mother had convinced her that time was fleeting and that she shouldn't waste any more of it. Roselin had an ulterior motive. She wanted to see her daughter in a committed relationship before she died. She wanted to make sure that Brett would have a family, and that family would include Taylor. Taylor needed a commitment, and Brett needed the support of a loving partner.

The movie, a comedy that completely missed the mark, was totally dismal, and the two women walked back to the car, hands linked as they shared their disappointment. Brett and Taylor made the quick trip back to the house in comfortable silence. They walked into the house together before Brett spoke.

"Would you like to sit out on the back deck with me for a little bit? It's not too cold and the moon is full."

"Sure, honey." Brett led the way to the back deck where a padded bench sat facing the cloud-shrouded mountains.

Brett held tightly to Taylor's hand as they sat down. She turned to face Taylor. "I wanted to thank you for being completely understanding with everything while I'm trying to get things together. I'm sorry about last night. I never want to disappoint you."

"Brett, you're doing just fine. I know this is hard for you. I want to be there for you. How could I do otherwise? I love you."

It was that simple statement that made the words in Brett's heart bubble out. "I love you so much, and I've learned that life can change overnight. I don't want to wait any longer to ask you something."

"What honey?"

"I want a life with you. I know your business is very important to you and I'd be willing to live anywhere you want. I'll love you for the rest of your life and I promise always to be faithful. I know you want children, and I promise to be a good parent. Will you marry me, please?"

Taylor was so overwhelmed and surprised by Brett's hastily spoken and unexpected proposal that she burst into tears, much to Brett's astonishment. But she was able to respond without hesitation. "I love you, Brett. I want to marry you and live with you. I would love to raise children with you. Yes, I will marry you."

Brett heard only the word *yes*, and she was elated. She wrapped her arms around Taylor and kissed her, every bit of love in her heart poured out in that one kiss. It was a long time before either woman pulled away.

"Taylor, I have something for you. If you don't like it I won't be offended, but I wanted to be traditional and a little bit old-fashioned. It's important that you know how much you mean to me."

"I know, honey." Taylor's face was streaked with tears as she listened to Brett.

Brett slipped slowly to her knees in front of Taylor and handed her the ring box, her eyes glistening with her own tears as she waited for Taylor to open the box. Taylor knew how painful kneeling was for Brett but she remained kneeling waiting for Taylor to look at the ring. She opened the black velvet box and gasped. If she had ever asked for a diamond ring, it would have been this very one, stunning in its simple setting. It was sparkling brilliantly, each facet cut to perfection to enhance the blue-white coloration. Taylor would have been happy if it had been a plain gold band.

"It's perfect, honey, so very perfect, just like you." She leaned over and kissed Brett softly, telling her with her lips just how much she loved her. "Now, would you please get up off your knees? I know that has to be painful."

Awkwardly, Brett stood up, grinning happily as she pulled Taylor up into her arms. "This is what I was shopping for yesterday. I would have taken you with me otherwise. I wanted to surprise you, and it was worth it! Can you stand a little more news?"

"What?"

"Do you want to take a quick trip with me to New York in a couple of weeks? The U.S. Ski Team has asked me to be the coach of the Olympic team. Their representative called me today and we spoke for quite awhile. They're willing to move the training center to Boulder if I take the job—that is, if you agree that I should take the job."

"Do you want the job?"

"Yes, but not if it gets in the way of us, you're more important than any job." Brett had learned a very valuable lesson. Taylor would always be the most important part of her life. She would make sure she kept nothing from her.

"If you want the job, I want you to take it."

"I love you, Taylor."

"I'm glad, because I love you so very much, and I'm so proud of you."

The two women kissed and then Brett slowly moved Taylor into the house, tugging on her hand. She pulled her all the way into her room and shut the door. She gently guided Taylor over to the side of her bed. Taylor still held the ring box open in her hand. Brett removed the ring from the box and placed the empty box on her night table. Then she turned to Taylor who waited breathlessly for Brett to slide the ring on her finger. Brett leaned over and kissed her ring finger softly then stood up and slipped the ring onto the third finger of Taylor's left hand.

Without a word, Taylor reached up and began to slide Brett's shirt up and off her body. She wanted to touch her so badly. She had been waiting an eternity for this moment. Brett shuddered as Taylor's hand touched her bare shoulders and caressed her back. They shared a kiss that increased in intensity as Brett's tongue moved hotly through Taylor's mouth. Taylor suckled on her tongue, forcing a moan from her as she rapidly unzipped Brett's pants and pushed her panties and slacks down in one smooth motion. She would wait no longer to touch her. Rachel's words echoed through Taylor's mind. She didn't let anyone touch her. Taylor would touch her and be the only woman to ever touch her again.

"I want to love you, honey. I'm going to be the only one to ever make love to you."

"Please, love me. It's been so long," Brett murmured, as her hands worked to remove Taylor's shirt and bra.

"Lie down, honey." Taylor pushed Brett back until she was flat on the bed. Then Taylor removed the rest of her clothes and slid gently onto Brett's naked body, resting on her arms as she looked down at Brett's face. Brett moaned as Taylor's hips nestled against hers. Taylor sighed and felt Brett's wet center against her thigh. She bent and pressed a kiss to Brett's throat and then her upper breast, as her lips whispered across the fragrant skin.

"I love your body. I missed you so much," Taylor breathed against Brett's mouth, and her fingers traced over her full breasts and squeezed her taut nipples. Her fingertip swirled around Brett's nipple, and then teased it with sexy little tugs. Her mouth found the other nipple and sucked heavily on it.

She teased the swollen peak with her teeth, as Brett cried out in pleasure. Rubbing her tongue back and forth, Taylor drove Brett crazy with her attentions. Brett's hips pushed up against Taylor's as she gasped.

"I'm going to come."

"Not yet, honey."

"Oh, please, it's been so long." Brett could barely speak; she was on the razor's edge of pleasure and pain.

"I know, but I want to taste you." Taylor's hand moved slowly over Brett's stomach stroking the skin just above the glistening black curls. She felt Brett's body vibrating underneath her and knew her lover was close. She rose up on her arms and slid down Brett's body until her mouth was above her wet center. She wanted more than anything to make perfect love to Brett. She bent and stroked her clitoris with her tongue.

"Oh God, please, Taylor, please."

Taylor surrounded Brett with her lips sucking her hard as her long fingers filled her deeply. "Now, honey, you can come now."

Taylor's fingers filled Brett tightly. Her body jerked and her hips arched against Taylor's wonderful mouth. Just as Brett's first orgasm finished rolling through her body, Taylor moved up her body, her fingers still deep inside Brett and she fit her hips over her hand, her mouth meeting Brett's in a kiss, her tongue tasting her. Her hips moved in the same rhythm as her tongue as she drove Brett up again into a blistering orgasm. Brett cried out once more and her arms trembled against Taylor's back. Brett began to cry, and Taylor kissed the hot tears away with soft, gentle kisses. She slowly removed her fingers and then held her as she wept.

"You're the only one that I've ever let love me like that."

"What do you mean?"

"You're the only one I ever let put her mouth on me. You were always the only one Taylor. It's always been just you, only you."

Taylor's body had been so ready for Brett's touch that her words alone made her come, and she cried out as her body shook against Brett's.

"I love you, Taylor." Brett gently rolled her onto her back as Taylor looked up at her.

Brett bent over the love of her life and met her lips in a kiss, one to cherish and one of hope and complete love. Her fingers caressed Taylor's breasts and teased her nipples, and her hips rocked against Taylor's in a rhythm as old as time. Taylor's hips arched up into Brett's as their bodies slid against each other in remembered moves. It had always been like this with them—as natural and as perfect as lovemaking could be.

Taylor felt her body began to fall, and she locked her fingers in Brett's hair and pulled her close in a kiss. She slid into her orgasm rapidly as it shimmered and sparkled its way through her body until she was incandescent with pleasure. "Brett, I'm …"

Brett moved her hips harder into Taylor until at last she went slack on the bed. Brett's head rested on her chest as she caught her breath. Taylor's hands moved to Brett's back, slowly stroking up and down. The need to touch Brett was still overwhelming.

Brett started move off Taylor, and Taylor's arms tightened around her. "Please stay on top of me. I like to feel the weight of you on me."

Brett reached up and met Taylor's mouth in a kiss, her tongue sliding against Taylor's upper lip before entering her mouth. Their mouths met in kiss after kiss as passion once again surged through their bodies.

Taylor became ravenous to touch Brett again, and her hand slid between their bodies and found her pulsing clitoris, swollen and hard. Taylor's fingers surrounded and squeezed, milking Brett until her head arched back and she groaned. Taylor drank in the vision of Brett succumbing to her orgasm. She was so sexy, so beautiful. Taylor felt her body react to Brett's vulnerability. Brett's hand slid between them and into Taylor, driving her immediately over the edge, crying out as she held Brett against her body.

In the aftermath of their intense experience, Taylor lifted her hand and looked at the ring glistening in the dark. She began to weep softly. "I'm going to marry you, honey. I'm going to love you for the rest of your life."

"Yes, you are." Brett clasped Taylor's left hand and kissed her finger next to the ring.

They slid into sleep still holding each other, unwilling for one moment to let each other go. They had been through so much to finally be together, and nothing would ever come between them again. Taylor knew beyond the shadow of a doubt that Brett would never sleep with another woman. She trusted her beyond belief and would do so for the rest of her life. She knew Brett would struggle with alcohol and the loss of her career, but she also knew that Brett would do her best to deal with it, and Taylor would be there for her.

Brett was first to wake and found Taylor tucked up against her back, her arm draped around her waist. She turned around to face Taylor, and her breath stopped in her chest as she watched her lover sleep. She felt tears slide down her cheek as she gazed at her beauty. She lay quietly watching Taylor for almost an hour, until Taylor's eyes fluttered open to find her lover watching her with love-filled eyes.

"Hi."

"Hi."

"This is for real, isn't it?"

"Yes, it is." Brett smiled and picked up Taylor's hand where the diamond sparkled and turned so Taylor could see it. "You are truly mine at last."

"Yes, I am, for the next hundred years or so."

"So when do you want to have a baby?" Brett asked as she snuggled up against Taylor.

Taylor couldn't help but laugh as she saw the childish delight on Brett's face. "Don't you think you ought to marry me before you get me pregnant?"

"We can have a commitment ceremony this weekend. I figure you could be pregnant within a month."

"A month?" Taylor's eyes opened wide as she looked at Brett in surprise. "I think we ought to wait a little bit longer than a month, but I think a commitment ceremony real soon is a requirement. I want your mother to be there."

"Yes, it's important that she knows I found my soul mate."

"I have the feeling she already knows that."

"So can we tell her that you've officially said yes?"

"Of course."

"I asked her for her blessing before I asked you to marry me."

"I'm glad."

Taylor ran her fingertips along Brett's face memorizing her smile as she spoke. "She loves you, Taylor."

"I love her."

"I'm going to miss her so much." Brett's eyes overflowed with tears.

"I know, honey. I'm so sorry." Taylor pulled Brett into her arms and held her tightly. There was no need for any more talking. They took strength from each other lying together in each other's arms. As long as they were together, they could handle anything life dealt them.

CHAPTER 16

▼

"Mother, may I speak with you?"

"Of course, Brett, come on in." Roselin saw her daughter's beaming face and her heart settled in her chest. She didn't have to be told her daughter had found her heart.

"Are you feeling okay?"

"I'm fine, sweetheart, just a little tired is all."

"I could use your help," Brett spoke softly as she took a seat on the side of her mother's bed. Roselin put down the book she was reading.

"With what?"

"I need you to help me plan a commitment ceremony. Taylor agreed to marry me."

Roselin's eyes filled with tears as she reached out for her daughter's hand. "I'm so happy for you both. I'd be more than pleased to help you."

"We don't want anything large or too fancy, just family and close friends, here in the back yard."

"That sounds perfect, honey. What do you want me to help with?"

"Could you help me choose what to wear and who to invite? I also need you to help us pick out the invitations." Brett wanted to include her mother as much as possible.

Roselin didn't know if she had the energy to accomplish these small tasks, but she would do as much as she could for her daughter. She hoped she lived long enough to see the ceremony.

"Mother, there's one other thing we'd like to ask of you."

"And that is?" Her daughter's dark brown eyes were so full of happiness. Roselin felt that she would be able to let go now. God could take her at any time and she would be ready.

"Would you give us both away?"

Roselin couldn't have been asked anything more special than giving her daughter and the woman she loved away. "Oh, honey, I would be honored."

"Good. I'll let you rest now. Taylor's going to stop in to visit in a little while. She had some calls to make. I'm going to go work out."

"Brett, I'm so very proud of you."

Brett turned in her mother's doorway, stopped, and then turned to face the woman she respected more than anyone. "That means everything to me. I'm not going to disappoint you and Taylor."

Her daughter left, and Roselin closed her eyes in thanks. She had lived long after her two husbands and it was time … time to let go and let God and nature take its course. Her daughter would be fine with Taylor watching over her. And she knew her daughter had rediscovered her strength. There was new determination in her voice. When Brett put her mind to something she couldn't fail.

Taylor called Jeb first to tell him the news. She was bubbling over with emotion. Close to tears, she waited impatiently for him to answer his telephone. He was her family and she had to share her happiness with him.

"Mind and Body Clinic and Spa, Jeb speaking."

"Hi."

"Well, hello partner."

"Jeb, Brett asked me to marry her."

"It's about time!" he teased. He had heard the tremor in Taylor's voice and knew she was close to tears. "You okay, sweetie?"

"I'm fine, just a little bit overwhelmed. Everything is happening so fast."

"But you're in love with her."

"And she's in love with me, but it's still overwhelming and I need your help."

"You name it. By the way, I'm very happy for you."

"You and Rex are my family I want you to be here with me."

"Name the date and time. We wouldn't miss it."

"I'll let you know just as soon as everything is firmed up. Anything I need to know about at work?"

"No, other than that the spa is booked solid for the next two weeks."

"You're kidding! That's good."

"Yeah, and the clinic is bursting out of its seams."

"So we should have an excellent quarter."

"We're having a record quarter, and that's what I want to talk to you about. I think we're due for some expansion."

"We talked about growing our space out."

"Yeah, but I'm thinking maybe a second space."

"You think it's time?"

"Yep, and I've already considered some locations."

"Good, let's hear them."

"I thought I could come to visit you and we could go over some ideas I've been tossing around in my head."

"That'll work. When do you want to visit?"

"How does Thursday sound?"

"This Thursday?"

"Yes, I can get a late flight out on Wednesday afternoon. Be there in time to take you and Brett to dinner. We can talk Thursday, and I can be home that evening."

"You can stay here. I'm sleeping in Brett's room, so you can have mine for the night. Roselin, Brett's mother, is living here now. She's not doing very well."

"How's Brett dealing with everything?"

"Okay, so far. She's had to deal with quite a lot in a short time."

"How's she doing with the alcohol?"

"She seems to be dealing with it. She actually doesn't talk much about it. I know she still wants to drink, but she's been handling it."

"I'll see if I can get some time alone with her. She might find it easier to talk to me than you about this. It's not going to go away over night. She's going to be struggling with her alcoholism for the rest of her life."

"I know. I would like it if you talked to her about it."

"So, you think Thursday will work? It won't disrupt Roselin too much?"

"Thursday is perfect. I'll talk to Brett as soon as she finishes her workout. Roselin will be fine."

"I thought you worked out with her?"

"Only three days a week. She wants to learn to do it herself, so once a week I check on her program. She's also eating very healthy food even though her first choice would be chips and salsa." Taylor started chuckling.

"And you aren't cashing your checks from Mrs. Camden."

"How do you know?"

"She's sending them to me."

"I can't take money from Brett's mother, especially since I'm going to marry her daughter. Please don't cash them. I'll pay you back for my time."

"You sure as hell aren't going to pay me, and I'm not going to cash them," Jeb laughed. "She sure is persuasive."

"So is her daughter," Taylor admitted with a grin.

"I'll e-mail you my flight information."

"I'll pick you up and make reservations for dinner."

"I miss you, partner."

"I miss you. See you Wednesday night."

"You bet."

Taylor was smiling when she headed upstairs to visit with Roselin. She knocked quietly on Roselin's bedroom door and entered when Roselin's faint voice invited her in.

"Hello, Taylor. Congratulations."

Taylor sat down on the chair next to Roselin's bed. She looked so pale, so weak, that Taylor caught her breath. "Thank you, Roselin, but I think you already suspected this might happen."

The tiny twinkle in Roselin's eye made Taylor laugh and reach out to grasp her hand, squeezing it with affection. "I only gave fate a little nudge. Taylor, I need to speak to you about something. I'm not going to last more than a month or so and I want so badly to see you and Brett celebrate your commitment. If you're agreeable, would you suggest to Brett that you plan your ceremony no later than a couple of weeks from now?"

"Roselin, I'm so sorry." Taylor couldn't keep from crying.

"Taylor, it's time sweetheart. But Brett is going to have difficulty accepting my death. I know I'm asking a lot of you, but can you help her? She's just getting back to being her old self and I don't want my passing to keep her from all that she's capable of. I know she's still struggling with alcohol, too."

"I'll always be there for Brett, I promise you that. I love her."

"I know you do, and she loves you."

"I'll talk to Brett this afternoon and suggest that we plan to have our ceremony in a couple of weeks." Taylor smiled. Roselin was an amazing woman. "My business partner, Jeb, is coming to visit for a day to go over some business opportunities with me. Roselin, he's a recovering alcoholic and is going to talk to Brett about what she's going through. He wants to make sure she knows he will help her if she needs it."

"That's good. I understand what she's dealing with. She will need all the support she can get. Is your business doing okay?"

"It's fine! It's bursting out at the seams. We're talking about expanding."

"I'm glad. My checks aren't being cashed."

"Roselin, I don't want to be paid for being here. I want to be with Brett and I just can't accept your money. I hope you understand."

"Taylor, I can't think of anyone else I would want my daughter to be with. I'm glad she met you."

Taylor blushed with embarrassment. "I love you and Brett."

"We love you. I want to thank you for moving your commitment ceremony up. I know that it isn't fair for me to ask that the two of you change your plans for me."

"Roselin, both of us want you to be there with us. What matters is that our family is there. I consider you family."

Roselin reached up and placed her hand against Taylor's cheek. "You're my family, too."

Taylor and Roselin had been talking for about thirty minutes when Taylor noticed Roselin's hand was trembling in hers. Her eyes were also drooping. "Taylor, I'm going to have to shorten your visit. I'm a little tired."

"I'm sorry. I shouldn't have stayed so long. Do you need anything?"

"No, sweetheart, I think I'll just take a short nap."

Taylor stood up and then bent down and kissed Roselin's pale, dry cheek before leaving her room. She closed the door and then leaned back against the wall as hot tears streamed down her face. She didn't have much family of her own, but Roselin was special to her and Taylor grieved over her impending loss. She had enormous respect for her and was hoping to have more time to spend with her. She also knew that Brett was unprepared to lose her mother, and Taylor was at a loss to find the best way to help her.

"Taylor, what's wrong? Is Roselin okay?" Fran came up to Taylor, concern on her face.

"Yes, but she's very tired so she's having a nap."

"She's not eating enough to keep a bird alive."

"I need to talk to Brett. We need to make arrangements for our commitment ceremony in the next couple of weeks. Roselin is certain she isn't going to live much longer and she wants to be there."

"You go talk to Brett. Helen and I will help with anything you need. We'll have a beautiful party."

"Thanks, Fran, I appreciate that very much."

"Go! Brett's trying to convince Helen to make hamburgers for dinner."

"The heathen!" Taylor grinned and headed down the stairs intent on stopping Brett from a total downfall from healthy eating. Besides, Taylor loved hamburgers. She entered the kitchen in time to see Helen agree to barbequing.

"Quit harassing Helen, she has her orders. You're to eat healthy meals. It's part of your therapy."

"But they're barbecued hamburgers with mushrooms." Brett reached out and gathered Taylor to her, sliding her arm around her waist. "Please?"

"Well, I do love a good hamburger." Taylor grinned at Helen. "Excellent!"

"Do you have a little bit of time? I need to talk to you about a couple of things."

The two women walked hand in hand into the living room and sat down on the couch. Brett turned to face Taylor and then leaned into her and whispered in her ear. "Do you think anyone would notice if we disappeared for an hour or two?"

Taylor's grin was so sexy. It was all Brett could do to not to drag her back into bed. "I think someone might notice. Brett, I need to talk to you about our commitment ceremony."

Brett's smile disappeared as she looked at Taylor. Oh God, she's changed her mind and doesn't want to get married. Brett trembled, and her heart lodged in her throat. Panic made her shake as she looked at Taylor.

"Honey, don't look so scared, I want to plan the ceremony in a couple of weeks."

"A couple of weeks?" Brett went from fear to shock.

"Honey, your mother asked me to talk to you about moving it up. She wants to make sure she's still feeling well enough to participate." Taylor picked up Brett's hand and kissed her fingers one by one before saying what she knew was going to hurt her. "Brett, your mom is failing very rapidly."

Brett's eyes filled with tears that spilled down her cheeks. She hated to think about her mother dying. She wasn't sure she could handle that along with everything else.

"I'm sorry, honey." Taylor wrapped her arms around Brett's neck and held her tightly.

"Are you okay with planning our ceremony so soon?" Brett's voice was uncertain.

"Brett, look at me, please. I love you. I will love you for the rest of our lives. I would marry you today. So my answer is yes. What I don't know about is everything else. My business is in Los Angeles, and I have to talk to Jeb about how I can live with you and still be his partner."

"Are you worried about money, because I can support you? I made a lot of money skiing, and my father left me an inheritance that I haven't really touched."

"Sweetheart, I'm not worried about money, but I can't just walk away from the business."

"We can live in Los Angeles."

"No, we can't. You're going to coach the U.S. Ski Team here in Boulder." Taylor responded with a shake of her head. There was no way she would let Brett give up her dreams of coaching.

"I don't have the job yet."

"You will. Honey, Jeb is coming to town Wednesday night and staying through Thursday. He wants to talk about the business. I also want Jeb and Rex to come to the ceremony. If we're planning something for a couple of weeks from now, I can let him know exactly when."

"So when shall it be?"

"What do you say to a week from this coming Saturday? Helen and Fran will handle the food and prepare the house. I can find something for your mother and me to wear this week and arrange to have someone come fix your mother's hair. That leaves you to find something for yourself to wear and get someone to perform the ceremony. And if you give me a list of friends and family to invite, I'll call everyone. That just leaves music and our vows."

Brett slowly relaxed as she listened to Taylor's calm recital of the list of tasks. She wasn't backing out. "Do you want to write our own vows?"

"I would like to, if you agree."

"I really want that to be something we do together."

"I'd like that very much. So what do you think about everything else?"

"I think it sounds perfect, and I'm really glad you didn't cancel on me." Brett may have had a smile on her face, but she was deadly serious.

"Brett, look at me, please. We're in this together for the rest of our lives. I didn't take this ring from you lightly. The minute I said yes, I made a promise to you. Trust in that, please." Taylor's blue eyes gazed back at Brett.

"I trust you. It's just so amazing that we found each other again. I love you so much."

"Good, now we need to talk about a ring for you."

"I'd like to have a wide gold band. I also have the wedding band that goes with your ring in my desk."

"Do you want to pick a ring out or do you trust me to choose?"

"I trust you."

"Do you like diamonds?"

"I do, but I am not the solitaire type."

"I think I can find something you'll like."

"If you pick it out, I'll love it."

"So, we're getting married a week from Saturday." Taylor leaned her forehead against Brett's as she spoke.

"Isn't that amazing?" Brett responded, and then slid her lips against Taylor's in a soft kiss. Silently they acknowledged the huge step they were taking and how very much it meant to both of them. It might not be a legal ceremony, but it was a commitment in front of family and friends and just as binding as any law could make it.

CHAPTER 17

▼

Jeb stepped through the airport gate and his eyes located Taylor immediately despite the crowds of people moving through the bustling airport. She was grinning from ear to ear, her stunning face glowing with happiness. Jeb couldn't have been more delighted. He wanted Taylor to find the one woman that could love her for the rest of her life. Brett had been that woman years earlier, but Taylor hadn't trusted her. Jeb had. He'd seen the look on Brett's face when she had shown up at the spa hoping to convince Taylor to see her. Jeb could remember that conversation as if it was yesterday.

"Jeb, could you talk to Taylor, please? I didn't sleep with any one else. I love Taylor." Brett had looked exhausted, her eyes red-rimmed and full of tears. She had shown up at Jeb's office after Taylor had refused to speak to her for the third time.

"Brett, I've tried to talk to her. She simply won't listen." Jeb had argued over and over with Taylor to give Brett a chance to explain. Taylor had refused to see her, and Jeb had finally given up. No amount of talking would make Taylor change her mind.

Brett's eyes spilled tears as she looked back at Jeb. "I really do love her, Jeb. I will love her for the rest of my life."

Jeb had watched as Brett left his office, her face a mask of pain and heartbreak. He couldn't understand why Taylor wouldn't agree even to see Brett. It had taken him over a year to get Taylor to admit that she was still in love with Brett and another year for her to tell him why she didn't trust her. Taylor had lost her family at such a young age that she had a huge need to feel secure in her life. Trust was also essential to Taylor's security, and Brett had, in Taylor's mind, fractured the trust. This had made Taylor harden her heart. She wouldn't survive another loss. It would kill her. Jeb had understood Taylor's deep-seated insecurities. What he didn't understand is why she wouldn't at least give Brett a chance to explain what happened. Now things were very different, and Jeb was thrilled for both women. It wasn't easy to find the right life partner, and he knew Taylor and Brett were perfect for each other.

"Hey, partner." Jeb reached out and hugged the tiny woman tightly. He didn't miss the tears that tracked down Taylor's face.

"I've missed you," Taylor whispered, as she held Jeb tightly.

"I've missed you. Is Brett with you?"

"She's out in the SUV waiting. Parking is a bitch around the airport. Besides, she wanted to give us some time to reconnect."

"Let me see that rock glistening on your finger."

Taylor lifted her hand up so Jeb could see her ring.

"Wow, Brett must really like you or something," Jeb teased, as he held Taylor's hand in his.

"She loves me." Taylor's smile was blazing.

"I take it you love her back."

"Totally."

"Taylor, you never stopped loving her." Jeb placed his hand on Taylor's shoulder.

"I was wrong, Jeb. Brett never slept with another woman. I believe her completely. When she commits herself to something or someone, it's a total commitment." Taylor had no more doubts about Brett. She knew deep in her heart that Brett was completely true to her.

"I'm very glad that you've found each other again." Taylor's smirk didn't go unnoticed by Jeb. "What?"

"I think you and Mrs. Camden conspired to do a little matchmaking."

Jeb's eyes twinkled back at Taylor, but he didn't respond as he wrapped an arm around her, his briefcase and overnight bag in his other hand. "Come on, let's get out of here. I'm hungry. I hope you have plans to feed me."

"Absolutely, we're taking you home. Helen has been slaving all afternoon to fix you a home-cooked meal. I thought it would be more relaxing to eat at Brett's home."

"Sounds perfect."

Taylor hugged Jeb again and started for the exit to the airport. As usual, the Boulder airport hosted a bustling crowd of visitors to the skiing and recreational center. They pushed and threaded their way through the crush until they made it to the pick up area. Brett saw them as they came through the door, and she stepped out of her car and moved around to meet them.

"Hey Jeb, welcome to Boulder."

"Brett, you look terrific. Give me a hug, girl." And she did. Her arms had gained muscle as well as her legs and the rest of her body. She stood straight, wearing a pair of faded jeans and a bright red polo shirt. Her grin was huge and her eyes glowed with happiness. She looked healthy and well loved.

Brett felt the tears fill her eyes as Jeb hugged her tightly and Taylor looked on with a big smile on her face. Brett had always liked Jeb. "I'm glad you're here. Taylor has missed you terribly."

Jeb was surprised at the change in Brett. She looked almost as healthy as she had four years earlier. If he didn't know better, he wouldn't have known she was injured, except for her slowed gait. "Yeah, but she has you. I'd say that was just about perfect."

Brett's smile was blinding. "That just about sums it up. Here, let me take your suitcase."

Jeb and Taylor climbed into the car and, after stowing Jeb's suitcase in the back, Brett slid into the driver's seat and began the short drive back to her home. Jeb and Taylor chatted about work and Rex until Brett pulled into the driveway.

"Welcome to our home," Brett announced, as she grabbed his suitcase and went up the stairs onto the wide front porch and the entrance to the large house. Jeb followed Taylor into the entry of the natural wood home built at the foot of the mountains. He was impressed with the contemporary open living room and country kitchen. It wasn't anything like Taylor's modern condominium. The place had the look of a professionally decorated home but with the added personal touches that made it warm and inviting. The oversized chairs and soft brown leather sofa were inviting. The walls were natural stained cedar planks, on which were hung large photographs of the mountains and the surrounding hills. Brett had recently put up a picture of herself skiing in a downhill race before her injury. Taylor was proud of Brett's being able to think about herself as an ex-skier. It was a major step in Brett's mental and physical recuperation. The open space included a large kitchen with granite counters and knotty pine cabinets. Copper pots and pans hung from an iron rack above the center island. A large open wooden stairwell led to the upper floor.

"Brett, I'll take Jeb up to his room. Why don't you check on your mother and see if she's up to having dinner with us?"

Twenty minutes later Jeb and Taylor were sitting on the back deck admiring the sweeping view of the snow-covered mountains and sipping on a superb Merlot. Brett hadn't returned from her mother's room.

"This is a beautiful place. It feels very warm and welcoming." Jeb commented as he took in the incredible view around him.

"Yes, it is. It feels like home. Boulder is a very comfortable place. It's nothing like Los Angeles. It's modern and everything but it just has a small town, outdoorsy feel to it that makes you feel welcome."

"You like living here?"

"I do, but I could live anywhere with Brett."

"I'm glad."

"So business is really as good as you said on the telephone?" Taylor couldn't keep the guilt out of her voice.

"Better, and stop worrying. Even though you're sorely missed, we're slogging along." Jeb rubbed Taylor's back affectionately.

"So, you said you had an idea about how to expand?"

"Yeah, what would you say to opening in another location instead of expanding in Los Angeles?"

"Where?"

"What would you think about here in Boulder?"

"You're kidding!" Taylor was amazed at the suggestion.

"No, I've already done some background checking and a preliminary market survey. This place could use a high-end rehab and spa facility. You could oversee the construction, be here for the opening, and then manage the new facility. That way you could stay here, and we can expand at the same time. What do you think?" Jeb had done more than research it. He had a well-documented plan in his briefcase. It was good, very good.

"Are you sure this makes good business sense?"

"Absolutely, and we have the cash. We need to invest it somewhere, and this place makes perfect sense. I've crunched some numbers, and I think we could get it to turn a profit by the end of the first year."

"Sooner, if you use me to endorse your new spa." Brett spoke softly from behind them. "I didn't mean to interrupt."

"You didn't." Jeb smiled and motioned for Brett to join them.

"Brett, you don't need to do something like that." Taylor reached out and clasped Brett's hand as she sat down.

"It probably won't carry much weight, but if I can help I will."

"So you think it's a good idea?"

"I think it's a very good idea." Brett hugged Taylor. "It keeps you here in Boulder."

"So, Taylor, it's up to you." Jeb grinned at his partner. He was quite sure he knew what her answer would be.

"I say let's go for it!" Taylor laughed and reached her other hand out to Jeb. "And let's have a toast to the success of the new venture!"

"We can talk about the details later. Brett, tell me about the coaching opportunity. It sounds interesting." Their easy conversation and frequent laughter drifted back to the house. All too soon, it seemed, Helen called them to dinner.

CHAPTER 18

▼

"Helen, dinner was marvelous. Do you think I could convince you to move to Los Angeles and cook for me and Rex?"

"I like it here just fine, thank you," replied Helen good-naturedly. She was busy clearing their empty dinner plates from the table.

Brett and Taylor both smiled, and Helen's happy face reflected her appreciation for the compliment. Taylor couldn't help but tease her long-time friend. "I think Rex might object to the competition."

"He loves a good meal. Now, how about telling me some of your plans for your ceremony?"

"It's going to be here a week from Saturday. The ceremony will be in the afternoon out in the backyard, if the weather allows. I've reserved you a room at the Radisson downtown for two nights, so you're expected here on Friday. Brett is in charge of the ceremony." Taylor's smile was tender as she looked at her girlfriend.

Brett squeezed her fingers and smiled back. "The ceremony is at four, and we have a local Lutheran minister blessing the vows. Jeb, we'd be honored if you and Rex would be our witnesses."

"We'd love to. What else can we do?"

"Not a thing, we have it all covered." Taylor sighed. Everything was coming together so beautifully.

"We'd like to do something for you two. Are you going on a honeymoon?"

"Not right now. We're going to stay here in town until Brett has to go to New York. Then we're going to take a couple of days off while we're there." Neither Brett nor Taylor wanted to leave Brett's mother while she was so ill.

"Brett, expand a little bit about this coaching job. They want you to coach the U.S. Ski team?"

"It's not a for-sure thing yet, but if I can get myself healthier and stronger, the U.S. Ski Association has asked me if I would consider coaching the 2006 U.S. Olympic Ski Team. The Olympic committee has to review their petition for me to coach. If they approve, then an offer can be made."

"Brett says you're working yourself like a demon."

"She's a tough boss," Brett laughed.

"I am awfully glad you're doing so well, Brett."

Brett picked up Taylor's hand and kissed it tenderly before responding. "I had good reason to get my act together."

"I'm going to go check on Roselin. I'll be right back." Taylor bent and kissed Brett and then stood up and slipped out of the room.

Brett turned and grinned at Jeb. "She wants me to talk to you about being an alcoholic."

"I figured that," Jeb chuckled. "How're you doing?"

"Right now I seem to be doing okay. I don't miss it most of the time, and then out of the blue I feel like having a drink."

"What do you do when you feel like that?"

"I usually go work out."

"Brett, you might want to look into attending AA meetings for a while. They provide a support mechanism to fall back on."

"I've thought about that. Do you still go to meetings?"

"Occasionally, usually when I'm stressed or dealing with something important. And Brett, you can call me anytime, anywhere. I'll always be there." He knew what it was like when an alcoholic first gave up her crutch. Everything would be fine until something happened that created a large amount of stress. That's when most alcoholics fell off the wagon. He wanted Brett to know that he could be called upon to help.

"Thanks, I appreciate that very much."

Jeb reached out and placed his hand on Brett's. "Taylor adores you, and I saw something very special in you years ago. You're going to be fine."

"Thanks, I know I'm very, very lucky."

"Brett, you had to work like hell to get where you are, luck had nothing to do with it. I do need to explain something to you about Taylor. She may not have given you a lot of detail about her life. She knows just how hard it is to recover from life-altering injuries. When she lost her parents and was hospitalized, alone and afraid, it was the kindness of a physical therapist and her husband that helped

Taylor survive. All Taylor ever wanted in her life was a family—a lover who would always be there. She needs that most of all."

"She still doesn't trust me completely," Brett whispered softly, her eyes full of hurt.

"She's trying to overcome years of being afraid of being left alone. Be patient with her."

"Jeb, I need you to know that I never ever cheated on Taylor when we were dating."

"Honey, I know you didn't, but Taylor couldn't see beyond the rumors and your reputation. You'll have to deal with all of that some day."

"She is my life."

"Brett, you are hers, and she's still got deep seated fears of losing someone she loves. Losing her parents at such a young age had a profound effect on her. That has nothing to do with you. It's Taylor's way of protecting herself."

Brett remained silent absorbing his words. Jeb sat back and waited for Brett to react.

"She told me when we first got together that she wanted to have a couple of children."

"She still does."

"I've always wanted to be with someone who wanted to raise children."

"Have you told her?"

"Yes, but I'm not sure she thought I was completely serious."

"Maybe you should talk more to her about it."

"I think I will."

Taylor's light laughter could be heard from the second floor, and Jeb and Brett smiled at the sound. "She's happy here with you."

Brett's eyes filled with tears as she watched Taylor walk down the stairs, a big smile on her face. "Helen made your mother a bowl of popcorn, and she's watching a video in her room."

"She's feeling okay?" Brett asked, as Taylor sat down next to her and slid her hand into Brett's.

"She's having a good night. Why don't you go up and talk to her for a minute?"

"I think I will, and then I'm going to wander off to bed and leave you and Jeb to talk." Brett leaned into Taylor and brushed her mouth with a kiss, then lifted her fingers to her mouth and kissed the diamond on her hand. She stood up and slowly made her way to the stairs, her gait steady and without her usual limp.

Taylor's eyes stayed glued to her figure until she disappeared up the stairs. Jeb's eyes studied Taylor's amazing face. It pleased him no end to see the happiness in her gaze.

Taylor turned back to Jeb and blushed when she realized he had been watching her. "What?"

"You're toast, girl. And so is Brett."

Taylor's laugh was musical as she turned to face Jeb fully. "When do you want me to start looking for a place here in Boulder? Do you have any idea about size and location? How much money do we have for a remodel?"

"As a matter of fact, I have a full file in my briefcase to leave with you now that you've agreed to go ahead. I've gone over it with our accountant, and he thinks it's a sound plan, so why don't you go through everything and then we'll talk about next steps? I haven't put any thought into the actual interior work. You did such a great job on our current space I thought you might want to have a free hand with this place."

Taylor's watched Jeb carefully as she responded. "Are you sure this is what you want to do, expand in Boulder? Or are you just doing this because of me and Brett?"

"I'm doing this because it's a sound business decision, and you and I were already talking about expansion. Boulder is a great place for something like this."

"I don't want Brett to feel like she has to do anything to help us."

Jeb placed his hand on Taylor's as he spoke with compassion to his best friend. "Taylor, she wants to help because it's yours. Let her do what she can to help you. She wants to be your partner in all things. That includes making sure she's supportive of your business life. You need to let her do that. It's part of trusting her."

"She needs to expend all her energy on recovery and dealing with her mother's illness."

"She will, honey. She also needs to be a part of your life, business and otherwise." Jeb hugged Taylor tightly. "I'm going to get the file for you and then get to bed. We can talk some more tomorrow before my flight out, and right now I need my beauty sleep."

Taylor snorted with laughter. Jeb was gorgeous no matter what he did. "Do you remember where your room is?"

"Yes, Mom." Jeb flashed a grin, as he rose from the couch and went to where his briefcase sat by the dining room table. He pulled a thick file out and handed it over to Taylor.

"Whoa, you have done a lot of work."

"I was bored and needed a challenge." Jeb turned and started for the stairs. "Besides, it's a fantastic idea, even if I thought of it."

Taylor snorted with humor as she responded. "Goodnight."

"Goodnight, sweetie."

Taylor stood up and carried the file with her into Brett's bedroom. She placed the packet on the desk and then grabbed her nightshirt and headed for the bathroom to get ready for bed. She hummed softly to herself as she washed her face and brushed her teeth, her thoughts focused on what she needed to accomplish the following day. She had no awareness of Brett standing in the doorway watching her with a slight smile on her face.

"Oh, Brett, you startled me, honey."

"You're enjoying Jeb's visit?"

"Very much." Taylor leaned against the sink, watching her lover.

"Are you really going to open another spa here?"

"Yes, if you think it's a good idea."

"I want you to do what makes you happy."

"I am. I'm marrying you."

"Taylor, I want to know if you still want to have children?"

Taylor's smile froze on her face, as her heart thumped loudly in her chest. "I'd like to, but if you don't think it's a good idea, we don't have to."

Brett moved slowly into the bathroom, her eyes locked onto Taylor's face. She stopped just inches away from Taylor. The heat from Taylor's body made her want to groan as passion flared in her own body. She raised her right hand and placed it gently against Taylor's face. "I'd like to have two that look just like you."

Taylor couldn't stop the tears as Brett covered her mouth with a kiss, telling her with her mouth just how much she treasured her. It took them both under. Murmurs of love and need filled the bathroom. Taylor wrapped her arms around Brett and held her tightly, and Brett's mouth returned to hers again and again.

"I need to love you, honey," Taylor spoke against Brett's neck as her teeth gently bit the side of her neck.

Without a word, Brett turned and pulled Taylor into the bedroom and next to their bed. Wordlessly, she removed Taylor's nightshirt and then stood gazing at her naked body with hunger so strong she thought it would choke her. For years she had wanted Taylor, needed Taylor, and now possession overwhelmed her.

Taylor felt Brett's eyes slowly travel over her body like a caress, and it made her tremble. No one had ever looked at her with such yearning. "I love you, Brett."

Brett's smile was full and her eyes lit up as she gently pushed Taylor backwards onto the bed. She bent over and her mouth unerringly found Taylor's wet and hard center, tasting the sweet flavor of her lover.

"Brett …"

Brett's teeth and tongue stroked and teased Taylor until she was close to exploding. Brett knew her lover's body well and kept her on a razor's edge until Taylor was frantic for release.

"Now, honey, please …"

Brett's shoved two fingers deeply into Taylor as she slid her tongue against her clitoris. The orgasm slammed through Taylor's body, and she cried out with pleasure, her body arching up against Brett's mouth. Again, Brett filled her and stroked deeply inside her. Another wave surged through Taylor making her shudder. She grew slack on the bed, her chest heaving as she tried to catch her breath. Brett moved up Taylor's body and lay down next to her gathering her against her still fully clothed body. She placed her face against Taylor's, holding her gently as her body calmed down. It was several minutes before Taylor was able to do anything but gasp. She turned until she was facing Brett and nuzzled her with lips against her cheek.

"You positively drained me."

Brett chuckled quietly. "I did, didn't I?"

Taylor's fingers worked their way under Brett's shirt and tugged it out of her jeans and slid it up off her shoulders and over her head. "You're way overdressed."

"Yeah, how about I take care of that?"

Brett quickly jumped up and shucked off the rest of her clothes, leaving them in a pile on the floor. She lay down on her back on the bed next to Taylor. Taylor slid her thigh over Brett's hips pulling her close as she ran her hand across her firm stomach and ribs.

"You know I've always loved your body. The first time I saw you naked you took my breath away. But now when I look at you with all of the scars from your surgery, I think you are more beautiful than ever. I'm so proud of you." Taylor's fingers slid lightly over Brett's shoulders and arms savoring the firmness that was becoming more pronounced every day. Brett laid quietly watching Taylor's face as she took her time loving Brett. This was the lovemaking that Brett had locked into her heart after being with Taylor the very first time. She couldn't forget how Taylor had taken her time as if she was cherishing every moment. Taylor rolled up and bent over Brett's body, surrounding her nipple with her lips and sucking it into her hot mouth.

Taylor's fingertips traced over her breasts, and Brett moaned, her nipples aching to be touched. Her body began to tremble as she restrained herself, letting Taylor set the pace.

"Oh, God ..."

While Taylor tasted and savored both breasts, her fingertips traced down Brett's slim thighs and over her hips. The she brushed the dark curls between Brett's thighs and barely touched her wet center. She loved touching Brett this way, loving her completely. Her fingers found Brett's clitoris swollen and hard, and she slid her fingertip against it, just enough to tease.

"Taylor, please ..."

Taylor smiled and tucked her face against Brett's as her fingers stroked her harder, her other arm tucked around Brett's shoulders. Brett's breathing grew ragged, and her hips churned on the bed as her body drew closer and closer to exploding. She reached down with her left hand and surrounded Taylor's wrist holding her as she continued to tease Brett.

"That's it, honey, let me love you." Taylor breathed her words against Brett's face, knowing that Brett was close to an orgasm.

"Taylor, I love you."

Taylor slid her fingers deep into Brett. Her thumb circled Brett's clitoris, once, twice, and Brett was undone. Brett cried out in pleasure, her body shook, her head fell back, and her eyes closed. Taylor watched the climax move across her face, and fell in love with Brett all over again. Brett slowly relaxed and turned into Taylor's body, burying her face in Taylor's breasts. Taylor felt moisture against her body and reached down, lifting Brett's face up so she could see her.

"Honey, why are you crying?"

Brett's face was streaked with tears, her eyes dark with emotion. "I love you so much, it's overwhelming. My life is perfection."

Taylor's own eyes welled up. "I feel the same way. We're very lucky to have found each other again."

Brett wrapped her arms around Taylor and sighed softly. "I think I could stay right here for the rest of my life."

Brett fell asleep within moments of speaking, and Taylor watched her for a few minutes before covering them both with the comforter and surrendering to a night of rest.

CHAPTER 19

▼

The morning of the commitment ceremony, the weather was clear and sunny guaranteeing an outdoor event. Taylor and Brett awakened early and helped Helen and Fran with the food, the flowers, and the decorations. By two o'clock, everything was in readiness, and Taylor was helping Roselin into her dress. Roselin was feeling very weak and found it difficult to help with anything. She was in constant pain and could barely get out of bed, but she was determined that nothing would keep her from watching her daughter and Taylor commit themselves to one another.

"Roselin, are you going to be okay?" Taylor took in the pale face and trembling hands.

"I'll be fine, Taylor. Go get dressed. Tell Helen to come up in about thirty minutes to help me down the stairs. Go, you need to get ready."

"Roselin, I want to assure you that I love Brett very much and I promise you I will take care of her for the rest of her life."

Roselin's eyes filled with tears as she gathered Taylor's hands in her own. "I know you will, and I know Brett will take care of you. I have no doubt that the two of you were meant to be partners."

"Thank you for bringing us back together."

"Taylor, I only got you into the same house. Your hearts did the rest. Now go before Brett thinks you've gotten lost."

Roselin waited for Taylor to leave before lying back down on her bed. She just wanted to close her eyes and go to sleep, letting all the pain go. "Just a little while longer," she whispered, as she closed her eyes and rested.

Taylor raced down the stairs and almost collided with Fran. "Sorry Fran, where's Helen?"

"She's getting dressed."

"You look very nice." And she did. She was wearing a long floral-patterned dress. Her ash brown hair was pinned up on her head.

"Thanks, you need to go get dressed yourself."

"You don't think I can get away with sweats and a tee shirt?" Taylor teased.

"Brett wouldn't care what you wore." Fran grinned.

"Could you have Helen go up and get Roselin in about thirty minutes? She's dressed and ready, but she's going to rest until the ceremony."

"I'll tell her. Get going! Everything's been taken care of."

"Where's your husband?"

"He's outside pinning the last of the roses onto the arbor." Fran's husband had built the arbor and planted the climbing roses in pots, weaving them up and over the arbor so they would surround the two women.

"He did a beautiful job on the rose arbor."

"He is pretty handy. I think I'll keep him," Fran chuckled as she gently pushed Taylor. "Go get ready."

Taylor flashed another grin and quickly headed for Brett's bedroom. She had less than an hour to be dressed and prepared to say her vows to Brett. She entered the room and stopped dead in her tracks at the sight of Brett standing just outside the bathroom. Her black hair was glossy with good health, and her face was filled with happiness. She was wearing a cream-colored linen suit over a pale yellow silk blouse. Her shoes were soft brown leather, the same color as her belt. She looked sexy, excited, and most of all healthy.

"You look fantastic," Taylor whispered, as she stared at her lover.

"Thanks, and you'd better hurry. Rex and Jeb will be here in about twenty minutes, and the rest of our guests shortly after that."

"I know. It took longer than I expected to help your mother dress."

"Is she okay?" Brett's expression reflected concern.

"She's very weak but she'll make it through our ceremony."

Brett held her breath to rein in her emotions. She was on the verge of crying and had been most of the morning. "I'll go check on things and let you have the bathroom and bedroom all to yourself."

"Thanks honey. Do you have the rings for Jeb and Rex?"

"Yes," replied Brett, patting her jacket pocket.

"I'll see you shortly." Taylor moved past Brett, touching her hand briefly as she entered the bathroom and shut the door.

Brett sighed, turned away from her, and went to take care of a few last minute details. She needed to get the flowers out of the refrigerator, for one. As she crossed the large living room, Jeb and Rex stepped through the front door. Both men were wearing black tuxedos and looked extremely handsome.

"Hey guys, come on in. Taylor is running a little behind in dressing, so Fran, Helen, and I will have to entertain you."

"You look fantastic, Brett." Rex hugged her tightly. He was so glad to see how well she looked. There was no sign of a limp, and her left arm had regained almost all of its movement.

Jeb hugged Brett hello and wished her well on this special day. Then all three of them went into the kitchen to help Fran display the rest of the flower arrangements. They were all standing in the kitchen area when Rex's eyes grew big and he stopped talking. Brett turned to see what had him so surprised. Taylor stood just outside the far bedroom door in a turquoise gown that clung to her body like a second skin. The dress had thin spaghetti straps and an enticingly low bodice that revealed her full breasts. Her hair was swept up on her head in a cluster of curls, held back with delicate hairpins that sparkled like diamonds. She wore matching heels that gave her a couple of inches in height and made her shapely legs appear even more beautiful through the slit in her gown. She stood still watching Brett gaze back at her.

Brett's eyes never left her as she walked slowly up to Taylor and stood directly in front of her. She reached out and placed her hand gently against Taylor's cheek as she spoke.

"I've never seen anyone more beautiful than you."

"You are."

"You look incredible."

"So do you."

"I love you, Taylor."

"Good thing, because I'm mad about you." Taylor's smile was for Brett alone, as they drank each other in. It was indeed a moment to remember. "Helen, you should go get Brett's mother."

"I'll go, Helen," Brett responded, still smiling at Taylor. "I'd like to bring her downstairs."

Taylor watched as Brett turned away and began to climb the stairs, no apparent limp in her stride. Then she approached Rex and Jeb. "You guys look gorgeous."

"Thank you, honey. But I have to tell you, I don't think I've ever seen you looking this beautiful."

"Thanks, Rex."

"I thought Brett was going to swallow her tongue," Jeb teased as he hugged his partner and best friend.

"Wait until she sees what I got for later," Taylor laughed.

Brett knocked quietly on her mother's door. "Come in."

Brett entered the room and found her mother slowly sitting up on the side of the bed. It broke Brett's heart to see how much her mother had changed as a result of her illness. Her skin was translucent, her hair thin, and her eyes were dull with pain. What she wouldn't give to make her mother well again. It broke her heart that she had wasted so much of her time with her mother. She would give anything to have all that time back.

"Are you ready, Mother?"

"Yes, honey. You look very nice."

"Thanks, so do you." Brett helped her mother to her feet and supported her as she moved out of the bedroom and made her way down the stairs. She was going to find her mother a chair for the ceremony. Roselin was too weak and unsteady to stand for any length of time.

Jeb met them at the foot of the stairs and graciously took Roselin's other arm. He walked with them outside to the waiting rose arbor in front of the white folding chairs that had been set up for guests. The back yard was freshly mowed providing a carpet of green grass and the rose arbor had been placed in front of the chairs and was draped with pale yellow climbing roses. It was a breathtaking setting with the mountains in the background. Jeb waited until Roselin was settled in her chair, and then sat down next to her to keep her company. Taylor came out with a yellow rose corsage, and Brett pinned it to her mother's dress, then kissed her on the cheek. Helen and Fran snapped pictures. They had volunteered to take photographs of the occasion. Then Taylor and Brett pinned boutonnières on Rex and Jeb. Finally, Brett kneeled in front of her mother so she could pin her corsage on her jacket.

It was a poignant moment for everyone when Roselin began to cry. "I've waited so much of my life for this moment, and I'm so proud of you. Taylor will be as much my daughter as you are, and I know you'll both have a long, full life together."

Brett wiped the tears off her face as her mother kissed her gently. Taylor approached Jeb and smiled up at him. "You're my best friend and family, would you pin my corsage on?"

"I'd be honored, honey." Jeb finished pinning the flowers to Taylor's thin shoulder strap then wrapped his arms around her and hugged her tightly. "I'm so happy for you."

"I'm positively ecstatic and completely overwhelmed at how everything has turned out."

Within thirty minutes there were about twenty people milling around at the house, all close friends of Roselin and Brett. Even Rachel had been invited, showing up on the arm of a rather stunning dark haired woman wearing a suit and tie. Rachel went up to the wedding couple and gave them both a hug.

"Congratulations you two. You both look pretty terrific."

"So do you. We're glad you were able to attend. Why don't you introduce your friend?"

Rachel blushed and turned to the tall woman at her side. "Taylor and Brett, this is Kate Turner. Kate, meet Taylor and Brett, the lucky couple."

"Congratulations." Kate's voice was robust, her grin wide as she shook both of their hands in greeting.

"Thanks, we're glad you could make it."

"I'm trying to talk Rachel into a commitment ceremony." Kate's dark hair was cut short, her brown eyes large and gentle, and her arm wrapped snugly around Rachel's waist.

Rachel blushed and slid her arm familiarly around Kate's back as she looked at Brett and Taylor. "We just decided to become a couple. I thought we should wait a little while before getting hitched."

Taylor grinned and leaned over so only Kate and Rachel could hear her speak. "Why wait? It's amazing to imagine being together for the rest of your lives."

Brett smiled and gathered Taylor's hand in her own. *Yeah, that was a pretty great feeling.*

The ceremony was short and sweet, and Brett and Taylor stood in front of their family and friends and pledged their love. Their vows were personal and meaningful as they pledged their lives to each another.

"I knew my life was not complete until I found you. I was waiting for the one woman who could make me whole. I have found that in you, Taylor. No matter what happens in my life you will be my partner in all things. I will love you and take care of you as long as I live. I will be forever grateful for the second chance I have to get things right."

Taylor nearly wept as she spoke the words she had composed from her heart. "I will always be by your side. I am so proud of you and what you have accomplished. You have given me something I have wanted my whole life, a love that I trust completely. I will love you and take care of you for the rest of your life. You make me feel safe and protected within your love."

Brett's mother gave them her blessing. "I have been lucky to have found love twice in my life. Brett, my daughter, nothing has pleased me more than when you told me you had found the love of your life. I am so proud of you. And Taylor, my daughter, you have been a blessing that I will cherish, and I know your love for my daughter is true and deep. May you both find strength and pleasure from each other for the rest of your lives. I wish you nothing but happiness."

There wasn't a single dry eye when the ceremony concluded with a kiss and a round of applause. Brett and Taylor were in a daze as everyone crowded around them to wish them well and congratulate them.

All they wanted was for everyone to leave so they could be alone together for the rest of the day. They were inseparable while their guests mingled and enjoyed the food, conversation, and happy ambience.

Taylor thought she would go crazy just standing next to Brett unable to touch her in the way she wanted to.

Brett leaned over, and her lips brushed Taylor's ear. She whispered quietly, "Can we get out of here yet?"

Taylor turned and kissed her lover softly shaking her head in frustration. "Just one more hour and then we'll take our leave."

Brett had booked them a suite at a local bed and breakfast for the night so they could have the evening completely to themselves.

Brett was a thoughtful and generous lover. Taylor was pleasantly surprised every day at the little things that Brett did to proclaim her love. She'd had Jeb pack up Taylor's desk and office paraphernalia and ship them to Boulder. While Taylor had been busy with the ceremony and the Boulder spa project, Brett had their suite's workout area divided by removable wall screens, separating the bedroom area from the workout area, and creating another office space for her desk and Taylor's. Then there was the walk-in closet that Brett had expanded so that Taylor's clothes could easily fit in. Every day there were gestures of love that made Taylor's already full heart overflow with love. Brett would call her on her cell phone at odd times of the day just to say *hello* or *I love you*, even if she was only in another room of the house. Her actions spoke louder than any words she could utter.

Taylor gazed around the room and stopped when she noticed Roselin's gaunt face. "Brett, I think we need to take your mother upstairs. I'm sure she's exhausted."

Brett turned and sighed as her eyes sought the face she loved so dearly. Rose-lin's mouth was tight with pain, her complexion waxy. She was sitting next to Rex who had not left her side for the last hour, finding the charming woman delightful. He knew of her illness and his compassionate heart wanted her to be as comfortable as possible. He caught Brett's eyes and, with a small motion of his head, communicated to her that Roselin needed to go upstairs.

"Will you come with me?"

"Of course, honey."

The two women approached Roselin and, as they got closer, her pain ravaged face relaxed for a moment expressing nothing more than love and delight for her daughter and Taylor. "Mother, we're going to head out pretty soon and thought maybe you could use a break from all this chaos."

"Thanks, honey, I think I would like to go upstairs for a while."

Rex stood up as Roselin struggled to her feet with a grimace of pain. "It's been a pleasure, Roselin."

"I enjoyed meeting you, Rex. Thanks for the entertaining company. Please give my regards to Jeb."

"I will." Rex felt his eyes fill with tears as he watched Roselin's face. He was amazed that she had stayed downstairs for most of the party. She was obviously in excruciating pain. He knew it was her love for her daughter and Taylor that made her stay and he was overwhelmed by her show of strength and love. He was very glad to have spent some time with the amazing woman.

Taylor slipped an arm around Roselin's waist as Brett supported her other side. They slowly made their way to the stairs and very carefully climbed them. Roselin's body trembled as she entered her bedroom and was finally able to sit on her bed. Without a word, Taylor busied herself removing her shoes and nylons, then her jacket and skirt.

"Mother, here's a warm washcloth. I'll wipe your face and then you can take a nap."

"Brett, I'm so happy for you and Taylor."

Brett gently washed her mother's face as Taylor pulled the covers over the frail woman. "I love you, Mother."

"As I do you and Taylor. I'm so proud of you both." Roselin began to nod off, while Brett and Taylor watched her body slowly relax.

Brett returned the washcloth to the bathroom and came out in time to see Taylor kissing her mother's cheek as she slept on unawares. The overwhelming emotion she felt filled her heart and she grew warm, as love for Taylor flooded every part of her. Brett bent and placed a kiss on her mother's forehead. They left the room, leaving the door slightly ajar in case Roselin needed to call for anything.

"I think it's time for us to leave." Taylor grinned at Brett as they walked through the still crowded living room. "Let's leave all this to Helen and Fran and make a run for it."

"Good idea. Our bags are already in the car."

"I'll go say goodbye to Rex and Jeb." While Taylor quickly hugged and kissed her friends, Brett located Helen.

"Helen, we're going to leave. Are you sure you don't mind that we take off for the night?"

Helen and Fran had been adamant that the two women get away for the evening. "We'll be fine. You two get out of here."

"Could you check on Mother for me?"

"I will, Brett."

"We can't thank you enough for today."

"We loved doing it. Fran and I couldn't be happier for the two of you." Helen enthusiastically hugged Brett and then Taylor.

"Thanks, we're pretty happy ourselves."

Brett and Taylor escaped in a mad rush to their car as the guests caught wind of their exit and pelted them with birdseed.

"It's going to take months to get all this seed out of the car," Brett mumbled, as she brushed it out of her hair.

"Well, at least yours didn't fall inside your clothes. I have seeds all over my breasts."

Brett's head snapped around and her eyes grew hot as she looked at Taylor's breasts barely covered by the top of her dress. Taylor was trying unsuccessfully to keep some of the seeds from falling any lower. "God, it's going to take too long to get to the bed and breakfast."

Taylor looked up at Brett and gave her a sexy, sultry look that all but melted Brett into a puddle. "Then you'd better hurry, because I can't wait much longer to touch you."

Taylor's hand on Brett's thigh was totally distracting as she navigated the crowded streets of Boulder trying to get to their destination in one piece. Her hunger for Taylor was all consuming, and it made her tremble.

"Stop, please! You're killing me here," Brett pleaded as Taylor's hand moved higher on her leg.

Taylor's hand stopped its progress but continued to radiate heat onto Brett's leg. Their first lovemaking after their commitment ceremony was very important to both women, and Brett was nervous and completely overwhelmed at how much she needed and wanted Taylor.

The check-in was excruciating. Taylor stood sealed to Brett's side while she signed the register and accepted their keys. They barely made it into the suite before Taylor turned and shoved Brett up against the closed door of their room. Neither woman noticed the large, elegantly decorated room or the antiques that filled it. The king-sized bed sat prominently in the center of a large, Oriental rug. But all that was ignored as they reached for one another.

"I can't wait any more," she groaned, as her hips ground against Brett's and her hands reached for her breasts.

"Oh, God, I can't either. Let me ... I need ..." Brett couldn't speak clearly as Taylor pulled her belt from her pants and unclasped them. Then her hand was between Brett's legs and her fingers were deep inside her. Her mouth covered Brett's with hot, slow kisses.

Brett felt her orgasm almost immediately. She cried out in pleasure while her lover brought her quickly to the brink. "I want my mouth on you!" Taylor gasped, spinning the two of them to the bed and shoving Brett onto her back.

Brett's slacks were roughly shoved down her legs. She was naked from the waist down, and Taylor's mouth found her quivering clitoris. "Jesus, God, oh my ..."

Taylor was relentless, driving Brett again and again until she was limp and unable to move. Then she slid up Brett's body and wrapped her arms around her, holding her tight as she shuddered once more in Taylor's embrace.

"You are trying to kill me," Brett whispered against Taylor's neck.

Taylor giggled and opened her eyes to see Brett gazing at her with humor. "I just needed to have you."

"Well, you had me."

"Yes, I did, and I plan to have you several more times tonight."

"So you love me mostly for my body?" Brett rolled over and began to slide Taylor's dress up her over legs so she could touch her skin.

"I love you for your body. I also love you for your generosity, your compassion, your competitive drive, and your heart." Taylor smiled up into the dark eyes that never left her face.

"The first thing I fell in love with was your eyes. They looked right into me. I thought you could see into my heart from the first moment. Next, it was your sense of humor. Your laugh made me want to laugh with you. Then I watched how you were with everyone around you—so open, so honest. I thought you were incredibly beautiful from the first moment I laid eyes on you, but my favorite memory was when you looked at me at the zoo, a cotton candy in your hand, and grinned at me. You said, 'I like this side of you, Brett.' I remember asking you what you meant and you said the Brett you saw that day was someone who could love deeply and mean it. I do love deeply, and I will love you for the rest of your life. I do not take my commitment to you lightly, and I want us to have children that will grow up with your strengths and talents."

Taylor began to cry as Brett kissed her slowly, a kiss of love, commitment, and passion ready to explode. It didn't take Brett long to remove all of Taylor's clothes and then the rest of her own as she covered Taylor's body from head to toe with kisses, tasting every inch of the woman she loved more than life.

"I want you on top of me, please." Taylor's arms tightened around Brett's back as Brett settled between her thighs and rocked against Taylor's wet center. Again Brett slid her hips harder against Taylor's and she smiled at the quiet gasp that escaped from Taylor. Their hips began to slide against each other in a rhythm they both felt. Taylor's breath became heavy, her hands slid down to pull Brett's hips more tightly against hers. She locked her legs around Brett's thighs opening herself fully. She watched Brett's face inches above her own.

The strength in Brett's arms had returned, and she arched away from Taylor's body and spoke. "Look how we're joined, Taylor. This is who we are—lovers, connected in the most perfect way."

Taylor's eyes moved down, and she saw their bodies sliding together. Her heart pounded as Brett reached between them and entered her fully. Using her hips she drove her fingers deeply into Taylor over and over until Taylor's muffled scream against Brett's shoulder proclaimed her climax. Brett collapsed on top of Taylor, trying to catch her breath.

"Honey, are you okay?" Taylor's hands stroked Brett's back as she tried to settle her own wildly racing heart.

"I think I died and went to heaven."

"Well, then, you have company, because you aren't going anywhere without me."

"That's perfect then." Brett drifted into sleep, still tightly locked in Taylor's embrace. Taylor smiled and tightened her hold on Brett, reached over and pulled the comforter over them, then closed her own eyes and went immediately to sleep.

CHAPTER 20

▼

Life became fairly settled for the couple after the ceremony. Brett continued her heavy workout schedule which had expanded to include running, much to Taylor's surprise. Taylor was kept busy reviewing properties and buildings in the Boulder area, looking for a good property in which to put their next spa. Roselin's pain had become manageable, and she seemed to be going through a period of remission. Everyone was happily living her life, ignoring for the moment the inevitable outcome of Roselin's condition.

The three women spent hours talking, laughing, and making memories to be shared long after Roselin's time was over. They were painfully aware of the fleeting nature of this time and didn't want to waste one moment of it.

One summer afternoon several weeks later, Taylor was sitting on the back deck enjoying the warm sunshine with Roselin when Brett rushed out and exclaimed excitedly, "Well, it's official! I'm the new U.S. Ski Team coach for the 2006 Olympics in Torino, Italy!"

"Oh, honey, congratulations! I'm so proud of you." Taylor hugged her partner tightly.

"Mother, what do you think?" Brett sat down on the chair next to her.

"I couldn't be happier for you. You'll do an excellent job."

"Thanks, I feel pretty good about it. I'm just a little worried about whether I'll be able to go up on the slopes again. I haven't been on a ski slope since my accident. My job will require it."

Taylor looked at her partner with compassion. She knew how hard that admission had been. "How about you and I take a hike tomorrow and go up the chairlift?"

Of course Taylor would understand. Brett responded quickly, "That sounds good. There's another thing I need to talk to you two about. They would like me to come to New York for a couple of days and meet the sponsors and sign all the paperwork."

"When do you need to be there?"

"Next week, Tuesday and Wednesday. I would fly out Monday and be back Thursday afternoon."

"We'll be fine, honey. Won't we, Roselin?"

"Of course."

"Are you sure?" Brett hated to leave either woman.

"We'll be fine. I'm taking Roselin to get her hair done on Tuesday so we won't miss you too badly." Taylor grinned and reached out to squeeze Brett's hand as she teased her. She wanted Brett to know that her trust in her was unwavering.

Brett grinned back and sat holding Taylor's hand. The three women discussed Brett's triumph in securing such a prestigious job and didn't go back inside until Helen announced that dinner was ready.

It wasn't until later that night that Brett and Taylor discussed her upcoming trip. Brett was brushing her teeth as Taylor sat on the toilet watching her. Brett had on a pair of red boxers and a tee shirt. Her newly muscular legs and arms made her look healthy and downright sexy.

"Honey, could you promise me one thing when you're in New York?" Taylor leaned her chin on her knees, where they were tucked against her chest. She was wearing a back silk nightshirt.

"Anything." Brett turned to face Taylor.

"Don't let any girl reporters get near you." Taylor's eyes teased, but Brett felt that there was still some underlying doubt in Taylor's mind.

She reached out and placed both hands around Taylor's beautiful face. "You have nothing to worry about. I love you completely and I wouldn't let anyone or anything come between us."

"I love you." Taylor looked up into the clear dark eyes that hid nothing from her.

"Then come to bed and prove it." Brett grinned, pulling Taylor up into her arms.

Taylor couldn't have been happier with their sex life. She and Brett didn't make love every night, but their lovemaking was frequent, healthy and passionate. What she valued most of all was the time they spent talking after they went to bed, sharing their dreams and fears. It was this time that cemented their relationship and made them stronger as a couple.

CHAPTER 21

▼

Taylor dropped Brett off at the airport with a hug, a passionate kiss, and a promise. "I'll miss you and we'll have a big reunion when you get back."

"Love you."

"I love you, honey, and I'm so proud of you."

Brett walked into the Boulder airport, her stride as strong as her confidence. She was wearing a pair of tan pants, a pale gold silk shirt, and a brown suede jacket. She looked professional and downright sexy. Brett was back, and she was going to prove to her mother, Taylor, and herself that she was the best ski coach in the world. Failure would not be an option. When Brett and Taylor had jumped off the chairlift at the very top of the ski slopes on Friday afternoon, all Brett felt was excitement--excitement at the thought of being involved in what she had loved her whole life, skiing. She missed skiing very much, but she had faced the fact that physically she would never be able to do it again. She could teach others how to be world-class skiers. Now she had another goal and that was to be the best ski coach she could be. She had a new dream and was about to embark on another career she could be proud of.

Taylor's eyes welled up with tears as she watched her partner and the love of her life head off to pursue her next dream. Nothing could have pleased Taylor more than to know that Brett was healing in both mind and body.

Two hours later, Taylor returned home and was surprised that Roselin wasn't waiting downstairs in her usual place. She headed upstairs and knocked on her bedroom door.

"Come in." Roselin's voice sounded weak.

"Roselin, are you okay?"

"Yes, Taylor, I'm just a little more tired than usual. Do you mind if we reschedule my hair appointment?"

"Of course not. Is there anything else I can do for you?" Taylor didn't like Roselin's coloring. She looked ashen.

"Tell me how Brett was when she left today."

"Confident, excited, and a little arrogant." Taylor sat on the side of the bed and placed her hand on Roselin's as she spoke.

"Ah, the Brett we both love."

Taylor couldn't keep from laughing as she smiled down at the astute woman. "Yes."

"She'll be a good coach."

"Yes, she will."

"Taylor, if you'll excuse me, I'm going to take a nap."

"Of course, Roselin." Taylor stood up and bent over kissing her gently.

Roselin reached up and patted her softly on her face. "I'm so lucky to have you in my family."

"I feel like I'm the lucky one." Taylor stood up and left the bedroom, her face drawn. She found Helen and Fran in the kitchen canning green beans from the little vegetable plot in the garden.

"Helen, Fran, have you noticed any changes in Roselin lately?"

"No, she still doesn't have much of an appetite, but she seems to have less pain lately."

"She's taking a nap upstairs and she looks way too pale. I'm worried about her."

"We'll check on her for you."

"I appreciate that. I'll be in my office if you need me."

Taylor entered her suite and headed to her desk where plans for the spa were laid out. She'd found an empty building in town that had once been a large warehouse. It needed a lot of work to get it into shape, but she had seen beyond its current sorry state to what she could create. She was going to call Jeb and discuss it with him. The price was right, and the space was even larger than they were looking for. And there was plenty of parking, a necessity to the business. The building was located in the heart of Boulder, near restaurants and local shops. Location was critical to becoming a part of the community. Boulder swelled in size during the winter but also had quite a bit of tourism during the rest of the year as people were drawn to the rusticism of the mountains and the numerous hiking trails. Taylor liked the fact that she was able to bring new business to the bustling city. She had spoken to the Chamber of Commerce, explaining the business proposal and what it would mean to the city. It would create at least twenty more jobs and increase revenue. Taylor was excited to get the project started.

While Taylor worked at her desk, Brett sat in first class on the plane preparing for her first meeting. She had been working like a madwoman for weeks. In her briefcase, she had a training plan, a fitness plan, and dietary recommendations. With Taylor's guidance, she had prepared a comprehensive mind and body approach to coaching, and the U.S. Olympic Committee had agreed to her suggestions. Now, all she had to do was convince the athletes, which would not be an easy feat.

She knew most of them, having competed with almost all of the women at one time or another. She had partied with many of the men and women. With some of the women she had done more than party. That was the sticky part. She wanted no one to come between her and Taylor. She was going to make sure her intentions were clear to everyone. Brett was not there to play around. She had a job to do and she planned on being a professional while she did it.

She laid her head back against her seat and closed her eyes, relaxing, as she thought of Taylor and their relationship. It was amazing how wonderful it felt to wake up every day with her, to go to sleep at night wrapped in her arms, to know that no matter what happened in their lives Taylor would always be there as her partner and lover. They rarely disagreed about anything of consequence, and most of Taylor's irritation with Brett was that she felt Brett was pushing herself too hard. Brett's stubborn nature had caused a few arguments, but both women were able to recognize what was important in their lives and quickly settled any disagreements. They talked about everything, and Brett found that sharing her fears with Taylor made them easier to deal with. She knew Taylor would help her with anything, and that knowledge made her feel invincible.

When Brett landed at LaGuardia Airport in New York, a liveried chauffeur met her as she exited of the terminal. He drove her to her elegant hotel in a long, black limousine. The meetings with the committee and some of the athletes would take place in the Grand Hyatt in downtown Manhattan over dinner. Brett had spent quite a bit of time in New York when she was still skiing, some of it in support of her sponsors and some of it playing in several of the many clubs in New York City. She knew the area well, but on this trip she had no desire to immerse herself in the nightlife. In fact, she had absolutely no interest in it.

A press conference announcing her new job was scheduled the next day after her meetings with the committee and the athletes. She freshened up in her room before heading downstairs to the dining room for the first meeting. Taylor had helped her choose her wardrobe, convincing Brett that her usual casual slacks and polo shirt would not work. Brett had taken her advice and was wearing a midnight blue silk suit with a mint green shell underneath. She felt good as she rode the elevator to the lobby and stepped out into the crowded room.

"Hello, stranger."

Brett froze at the all-too-familiar voice, her stomach rolling in response. "Hello, Juliet."

Brett stared at the woman she hadn't seen since the night of her fateful accident. Juliet was still as beautiful as ever, wearing a yellow dress and matching jacket, her briefcase under her arm. Brett was surprised to feel nothing but sadness. She realized that, on that fateful night, she had been using Juliet as much as Juliet had been using her. She could no more blame her for what happened than she could blame the mountain. Brett had made the unfortunate decision to drink and ski at the same time. The responsibility was hers, and she was now living with the consequences. It still was somewhat difficult to look at the woman who had seen her self–destruct, however.

"Brett, you look good." And Juliet meant it. She couldn't tell by looking at Brett that she had been in an accident. She looked more grown up, more professional than she had years earlier, but otherwise just as handsome and compelling. Juliet had always been attracted to the charismatic woman and even now she felt drawn to her.

"I am good." Brett and Juliet stood off to the side in the large hotel lobby talking while people streamed by them. The hotel lobby was large and packed with incoming and outgoing patrons. "What are you doing in New York?"

"I'm here on business. We have a client that's representing Nike, and we have a photo shoot here in New York." Juliet's voice trailed off. She didn't know what to say to Brett. She'd lived with her guilt so long that it was a part of her and now it loomed large as she looked at the woman she believed she had almost killed. "I'm sorry, Brett."

"Juliet, don't. Nothing was your fault. I take full responsibility for everything. I chose to drink, I put on my skis, and I'm the sole cause of my injuries." Brett spoke softly but directly.

"That's very generous...."

"I was angry for a long time and almost drank myself to death. Now, I just want to get on with my life and move forward."

"But ..."

"It's over, Juliet. Let it go. I have. I'm completely happy. I'm with Taylor Aronson now, and my life couldn't be more perfect."

Juliet smiled at the woman who still intrigued her. "Then I can only wish you a long and happy life."

"You too." Brett smiled. She was totally serene as she turned away eliminating one more ghost from her past life.

Long after Brett entered the restaurant, Juliet stood silently. She was processing the brief but poignant conversation. Maybe she could let everything go now that she knew Brett was going to be okay. She hadn't slept through a full night since the accident. Guilt and remorse had weighed heavily on her mind. She needed to change her own life, now, and move on. Maybe now that she had been forced to face her demons she could find her own happiness. She smiled as she realized she was happy for Brett. She deserved to be happy and well loved.

Brett took a huge deep breath as she approached the separate dining room where the meeting and dinner were being held. She was terribly nervous. She didn't notice the elegant ballroom or the people around her. Her thoughts were on her meeting and what she was going to say. Her cell phone vibrated in her pocket. She pulled it out and looked at the display. Taylor.

"Hi." Brett smiled as she answered the telephone.

"Hi honey, I just called to wish you luck with your meeting."

"Thanks, I'm just going into the room."

"Call me later and tell me all about it. You're going to be terrific!"

"I will. Taylor?"

"Yes, honey."

"I am the luckiest woman in the world."

"Oh baby, so am I."

"Love you."

Brett walked through the doorway with her head held high. She was the new coach. She didn't have anything to prove. She was born for the job. A slight grin played across her lips as she strode across the room and went to shake the hand of a member of the Olympics committee.

Brett's meeting went well. She was introduced to members of the committee and heard again and again of the faith they had in her coaching skills. She went over her plan and strategy with all of them, outlining her training and exercise program in detail. They nodded their heads as she explained how she intended to turn the program around. By the end of the meeting they were completely won over, and Brett was pleased with their reception.

By Wednesday morning she was prepared to meet with several of the athletes that would be under her tutelage. She'd had one interesting encounter during dinner the night before when a woman she used to party with on the ski circuit approached her table.

"Hey Brett, long time no see." Sheri's grin was full of mischief, her green eyes locked on Brett's face. She and Brett had had some crazy times in past years. They had skied and played hard, ending up in bed together several times after nights of drinking and dancing. Neither woman took their relationship seriously. They were just having fun. Sherri was a gifted slalom skier and a wild partier. Her golden brown hair curled loosely about her face, and she was still as cute as ever with her short, powerfully built body.

"Hello Sheri. How have you been?"

"Excellent! I'm looking forward to working with you this season." Sheri's emphasis on *working* hadn't slipped by Brett.

"I'm looking forward to a successful season myself. Sheri, I need you to know a few things. I take this coaching job very seriously. I'm not here to play around, drinking all night. I'm asking you to keep our relationship on a strictly professional level." Brett spoke clearly, her voice loud enough to be heard by several of the assistant coaches sitting around her at the table. They also needed to know what type of coach she intended to be.

"But, Brett …"

"No buts, Sheri. I'm going to say this only once. I'm here to do nothing but coach."

"You can coach and still have fun."

"I think I've made myself very clear. If you intend to play, please keep it quiet. If your ability to ski is in any way hampered by your lack of commitment, you and I are going to have serious words."

Sheri looked at Brett and nodded her head. "I get it."

"Good, because I intend for this team to bring home some gold medals." Brett lightened up her voice and smiled up at the surprised woman.

"I'd like that too." Sheri turned and exited the dining room.

"She's going to repeat what you just said to everyone," Tad Noble, one of her new assistant coaches, remarked.

"I know. I expected that." Brett grinned back at him. The message would get around very quickly. Brett wanted everyone to understand her commitment and her intent.

"There's a new sheriff in town," he laughed, turning back to his meal.

"Yes, there is," Brett chuckled, as she continued to eat her dinner.

CHAPTER 22

▼

"Helen, have you seen Roselin this morning?"

"I woke her up at nine and she asked me to bring her a cup of tea. I was just going to go up and see if she needed any help getting up."

"I'll go. I need to ask her something." Brett's birthday was coming up and Taylor needed some gift suggestions from her mother.

Taylor knocked softly on the door and then opened it. "Oh Roselin!"

Taylor hurried to the bed and bent over the silent form slumped on top of the covers. Taylor didn't need to be told she was gone. She spoke softly, "I'm so sorry Brett wasn't here, Roselin. I know she will miss you so much. So will I."

Taylor gently laid the woman flat on her bed and brushed her hair back from her peaceful face. She began to cry. "I'm so glad you aren't suffering any more, and I promise you Brett will be well taken care of."

Taylor hurried downstairs to talk to Helen. They had to call the doctor and the funeral home. She also had to call Brett. She didn't want to make that call. It would devastate her partner.

Brett reached for her cell phone as it vibrated on her hip while she walked out to get in her cab for the trip to the airport. Everything, including the press conference, had gone well, and she was expecting to start working with the athletes within four months in Boulder at their new state-of-the-art training facility. She was walking on air. Even the athletes had expressed support for her coaching methods. She couldn't wait to get started.

"Hi, honey."

"Brett, I have some bad news, honey."

"Mom ..." Brett's heart slammed in her chest.

"She's gone, sweetheart, I'm so sorry."

"Did she, did she …" Brett began to cry.

"She was in no pain. She slipped away early this morning."

"I'll get there as soon as possible."

"I know, love. We'll take care of her until you get here."

"Taylor, I …"

"I know baby, I love you too."

Brett sat in the first class section of the Boeing 757 in a state of shock. Her heart beat wildly as she realized that she had missed her mother's passing. It broke her heart that she hadn't been there for her, the one thing she wanted—no, needed—to do. God, she was such a failure as a daughter! "Can I get you anything to drink?" the flight attendant asked as she waited patiently in the aisle of the plane.

Brett looked up at the woman, her eyes full of pain and anger. "I'd like a glass of Scotch, neat, please."

By the time Brett got off of the plane she was completely inebriated and barely able to stay on her feet. Her body wasn't used to alcohol and was rebelling in a big way after only two drinks. Brett hadn't even thought of the consequences of her drinking. She had thought only of her mother and her own grief. By the time she had finished her first drink, she felt woozy. Her second had hit her harder. She couldn't think, she couldn't feel, and most of all she couldn't hurt.

Taylor spotted her as she came through the self-opening doors of the airport. She had tried to call Brett on her cell phone when she landed, but she hadn't answered. Something was wrong! Brett could barely walk. Her gait was unsteady. As she approached Taylor, Taylor could see her face and knew immediately what had happened.

"Brett, what, oh honey, no …" Brett's red-rimmed eyes looked at Taylor.

"I drank, Taylor. I'm so sorry. Please don't leave me. I'd be so lost without you." Brett's words were slurred. She was completely docile as Taylor bundled her into the car.

"I'm not leaving, sweetheart. We'll get you some help, I promise." Brett's eyes closed, and Taylor looked at her partner and cried—cried for the loss of Brett's mother and for her struggling daughter. She knew losing her mother was hard on Brett, but it hadn't occurred to her that she would turn to alcohol. She should have waited to tell her when she had gotten home.

By the time they arrived home, Brett was barely conscious. Helen and Fran had to help Taylor get Brett into bed where she slept heavily under Taylor's watchful eye. Taylor wasn't sure what the alcohol would do to Brett, and she was scared to death that Brett would continue to drink. Taylor had called Jeb immediately after Brett had effectively passed out, and he was on his way to Boulder. She knew that the next few days would be critical if Brett was to regain her sobriety. If anyone knew what she was dealing with it was Jeb, and Taylor needed help.

Brett stirred and then opened her eyes, her mouth so dry she couldn't swallow. Her head pounded and her stomach was nauseous. Then she remembered, "Oh God, Mother! I'm so sorry."

"Brett, honey, are you awake?"

Brett rolled her head over and her eyes met the concerned eyes of her lover. Taylor was sitting next to the bed where she had been watching over Brett for several hours as she slept. "Taylor, I'm sorry."

"Brett, listen to me. We're going to get through this together. Do you want to keep drinking?" Taylor spoke softly, her eyes locked onto Brett's face.

"No, I just was so angry that I wasn't here for Mother and I wasn't thinking clearly. I failed her."

"You didn't fail your mother. You were a wonderful daughter. She loved you. I understand how angry and sad you are, but we need to get the alcohol out of your system and then talk about what to do next, okay?"

"Okay. I love you, Taylor." Brett began to cry, sobbing as Taylor gathered her up in her arms and held her tightly.

"Everything will be okay, honey." Taylor held Brett until she was completely cried out, and then she helped her to the bathroom to take a shower.

By the time Brett was dressed, Taylor had made several telephone calls to finish the arrangements for Roselin's funeral. Everything had already been prearranged, and all she needed to do was take Brett to the funeral home to see her mother. Taylor was afraid that the visit would be too much for Brett in her fragile state, but she knew it had to be done.

Brett came out of their suite and came toward the dining room table where Taylor sat with Helen and Fran. She was still walking a little unsteadily. "Could I get a cup of coffee?"

"Certainly." Helen rushed to get Brett a cup as she sat down at the table next to Taylor.

The three women recognized the guilt and sorrow on Brett's face. Their hearts went out to the grieving woman. Taylor spoke softly to her. "Honey, do you want to see Roselin?"

Taylor had taken Brett's hand in hers, and Brett held on tightly. The bands in her chest loosened when she looked at her supportive friends. There was no blame or anger as they looked back at her. "Yes, I would."

"I'll take you this morning, and then we'll talk about the rest of the arrangements."

"Okay." Brett stood up on wobbly legs and then spoke again. "Thank you for taking such good care of my mother. I know she cared very much for all of you."

Helen responded, as Fran started to cry. "Brett, we loved your mother. It was an honor to take care of her."

Taylor stood up and tugged on Brett's arm. "Come on, honey."

The rest of day moved by quickly, and Brett dealt with the details, but her mind was a blur. The combination of alcohol and her grief made simple decisions difficult. She couldn't seem to see her way clearly. She was sitting out on the back deck staring up at the mountains when Jeb walked out the back door.

"Jeb, I didn't know you were coming." Brett looked up, surprised to see him.

"I thought you might need some support."

Brett hung her head in shame as she realized why he was there. "Taylor told you I got drunk."

"Yes, are you okay?"

"I don't know why I drank. It just happened."

"Honey, losing a mother is a very hard thing to deal with."

"I wasn't here for her."

"Oh Brett, you've been with her every single day. She loved you without reservation. Do you think she would be upset with you for not being here?"

Jeb placed an arm around Brett's shoulders when she started to cry. "I just feel so lost right now."

"I know, baby. But Taylor loves you and will be by your side, and Rex and I will always be here for you. You're not alone. We're all family."

Taylor watched as Brett allowed Jeb to console her. She needed someone who understood her grief and her weakness, and right now that someone was Jeb. They stayed out on the back deck for over an hour talking quietly. Then they came inside with an unexpected announcement.

"Taylor, Jeb and I are going out for an hour or so." Brett reached up and touched Taylor's forearm lightly. "We're going to an AA meeting."

Taylor knew how hard that statement was to make, and she masked her surprise. "Do you need company?"

"Not tonight, thanks, but maybe you can go with me some other time." Brett smiled as she spoke. She loved Taylor for her unqualified support.

"Okay, sweetie."

"I love you Taylor, and I promise I'll take care of this." Brett wrapped her arms around Taylor's neck and hugged her.

"I know you will." Taylor's gaze stayed on both Jeb and Brett as they exited the house. Taylor knew Brett would be just fine. Her resolve was firm, and Jeb was there to support and understand her.

Brett managed to get through the funeral with the support of Taylor and Jeb. She attended AA meetings every day for a week straight before she started to feel like she had a handle on things. Her mother had taken care of all the arrangements for her death, leaving all her worldly possessions to her only daughter. She had also left a letter to be read by Brett. It was that letter that strengthened Brett's resolve to deal with her problems with alcohol. She had read the letter with Taylor by her side.

"Brett, there has never been a mother as proud as I am. I watched you recover from your injuries and get your life together. You are an amazing woman with talent and heart. I leave this world knowing that you will garner many Olympic Gold medals for your efforts. I will be watching as you show the world how talented you really are.

I will also be watching as you and Taylor have my grandchildren. I know you will raise them with love and compassion, teaching them everything they will need to know about life.

Please do not grieve over my passing. I have had a full and wonderful life and I have no regrets. Take care of Taylor. I know she will take care of you and know that I love you dearly.

Your mother."

Brett cried as she finished reading the letter and then turned to Taylor. "I miss her so much."

"I know you do, honey but as she told you, she'll be watching over you."

"She always had such faith in me."

"That's because she knew you. There is nothing you can't do if you put your mind to it.

Brett smiled despite her sorrow and gathered Taylor closer to her. "Then I guess I better work to get you pregnant. She wanted grandchildren."

"I think that's a wonderful idea."

CHAPTER 23

▼

Three Years later …

"How are you feeling, Taylor?" Rex asked as he bent over her hospital bed where she lay serenely looking back at him.

"Pretty good, my labor pains aren't too bad yet. The doctor says it's going to be another couple of hours." Taylor was telling the truth. She looked radiant as she lay back against the pillows. The worst of her discomfort were the pains that arrived every thirty minutes or so, along with a lower back ache. Considering that she was soon going to deliver twin girls, she was feeling fairly calm. Her room was a private suite in the birthing center at the Boulder Hospital. The room was painted a soothing pale yellow, and soft background music wafted through the room. The bed covers were pale yellow to match the walls; there were no sterile hospital linens in this section of the hospital. The ambience was meant to keep expectant mothers comfortable as they prepared to bring new life into the world.

"Jeb's parking the car. He'll be up in a minute. Where are Helen and Fran?"

"They're down in the cafeteria getting a bite to eat. They brought me to the hospital and have been here for hours. They won't leave."

"Of course they won't. Have you talked to Brett?"

"No, I haven't been able to get through. It's hard to get her on the telephone lines in Torino. The hotel was swamped with incoming calls. I left a message at her hotel. She'll call me as soon as she's able to."

"She's going to be pissed that she's missing the delivery," Rex remarked with a grin as he sat in the chair next to her bed.

"Yeah, our timing could have been better but we talked about this possibility. Twins tend to arrive early." Taylor smiled happily up at Rex. She had found her pregnancy to be heavenly up to this point. Even with all that was going on in their lives, Taylor's being pregnant had been a joy to both of them. Brett had been joyous when Taylor became pregnant, and she loved it as her body changed with their growing children. Everything about the pregnancy excited and intrigued Brett. Finding out that they were having twin girls had almost overwhelmed her. She spent weeks getting the nursery ready before she had to leave for Italy and the Olympics. She had argued many a night that Taylor should reduce her workload at the spa and clinic. Taylor had stalwartly refused, driving Brett crazy. She had been working early that morning when her water broke, causing pandemonium at the spa.

"I can't believe how well you look! Pregnancy becomes you." Rex exclaimed as he gazed at Taylor. She positively glowed with health and happiness.

"Hah, you big flirt! I gained almost forty pounds!" Taylor laughed as she patted her protruding stomach. Thank God Brett thought her pregnant body was sexy. She had made Taylor send pictures of her stomach the last six weeks that she had been in Italy. She hated missing the last months of Taylor's pregnancy.

"Hey, beautiful, how goes it?" Jeb burst into the private birthing room, his arms full of flowers and two teddy bears.

"Good. It's going to be a while before these two girls arrive. Helen has a key to the house for you two. Your room is ready." Taylor and Brett had added on to the main floor of the house so the nursery would be connected to their bedroom. They had also added an office instead of continuing to use a part of their bedroom for that purpose. The upstairs still had two guest bedrooms, one exclusively for Rex and Jeb's visits.

"Hey, there's your girl!" All eyes turned to the television as the local newscaster showed an earlier telecast from the Olympic Games broadcast from Italy. The interview with Brett had been replayed all morning and afternoon. She was no longer just a local Boulder celebrity. She was now known worldwide as the charismatic and innovative coach for the U.S. Ski Team. Taylor's eyes misted with tears as she watched her ecstatic partner express her happiness over the U.S. Ski Team's complete sweep of the Winter Olympics. She had done it! Not only had the team taken more gold medals than ever before, Brett was being credited with turning the U.S. ski program around.

"She did it!" Taylor whispered her eyes full of pride and love for the woman who had overcome so much. "Her mother would be so proud."

"Just like we all are. They're saying that her unique program was the reason for their success. I wonder where she got all her advice about mind and body athletics," Jeb commented with a grin. Everyone knew that Taylor was as much a part of Brett's program as she was herself. They had collaborated on the development of her strength training and her physical therapy for the ski program.

"She knows what it takes. She's been through it all," Taylor responded, taking Jeb's hand and gasping as a labor pain caught her unawares.

"How're you doing, sweetie?" Jeb bent over and kissed her cheek. They were as close as ever. He and Rex spent many of their vacations over the last three years visiting Brett and Taylor in Boulder.

"Good, excited, nervous. I miss Brett," Taylor admitted as she breathed deeply to get through the pains.

"Honey, she would love to be here with you. You know you are her heart." Jeb held tightly to her hand as she closed her eyes. "It's killing her not to be with you."

"I know, it's been over a month and I miss her so much. God, I just need to hold her for minute. It's been so hard with the time difference and her grueling schedule. She barely gets any time to sleep."

"I know, sweetie, but she'll be home before you know it." He was aware that Brett had argued with Taylor for weeks about staying home from Torino to be with her for the births. Brett thought that Taylor and their children should come first. Taylor wouldn't hear of Brett missing her first Olympics and demanded that she go and fulfill her destiny. Jeb was keeping a secret for now. Brett was winging her way back home after receiving his telephone call. He had promised her he would call if Taylor went into labor. Brett wouldn't miss this occasion if she had anything at all to say about it. She had sworn him to secrecy, not wanting to get Taylor's hopes up if she didn't arrive in time. He knew she was about seven hours from landing in Boulder, and he was hoping Taylor wouldn't deliver before then. Six and a half hours later, Brett threw some cash at the driver and ran from the taxi, her small shoulder bag flapping behind her. She had left everything else in her hotel to be packed up by her assistant and sent home with all of the rest of their equipment. She hit the stairway at a gallop knowing that Taylor was on the third floor in the maternity wing. People jumped out of her way as she raced down the corridor. The message Jeb left on her cell phone had said that Taylor's delivery was imminent. She was breathing heavily as she burst into Taylor's room. She was delighted to find it filled with family and friends. Helen and Fran were on one side of the bed, and Rex and Jeb were on the other. Taylor lay in bed looking radiant as she relaxed between labor pains that were now about five minutes apart. Taylor had insisted on natural childbirth, and she and Brett had taken classes to prepare. Brett was scared to death.

"Brett, how, what ..." Taylor sputtered, looking at her frantic partner.

"I told you I wanted to be here." Brett grinned as she bent over the bed and kissed Taylor slowly, her hand grasping Taylor's as she felt the familiar heat and emotion fill her up. "God, I missed you."

"But I saw your interview earlier." Taylor was more than stunned as she hugged Brett tightly.

"They taped it yesterday so that I could get home quickly if I had to. I told them nothing would keep me away from the birth of our children. They understood," Brett whispered as she bent and kissed Taylor again.

"I'm so glad you're here." Taylor pulled Brett into another hug as she began to cry.

"So am I." Brett wiped her own face free of tears. "How are you feeling? Are the labor pains very close? What does the doctor have to say? What am I supposed to do?" Brett panicked as she realized how close the birth of her children was.

"Brett, honey, relax. Everything is fine. The pains are manageable. The doctor has been to see me several times, and I'm right on schedule. Sit here on the bed next to me. There's nothing to do until they decide to be born."

"What can I do?"

"Get ready to help me breathe. We'll be getting to the hard stuff soon enough."

Taylor couldn't have been more right. Within the hour Taylor was a minute apart with full-blown contractions as the babies demanded delivery. The room was cleared except for the doctor, Brett, and two nurses as Taylor prepared to deliver her twin girls. Brett leaned against Taylor's back, giving her support while she pressed down. The doctor guided the first child's head. She came out with a startled cry that announced her birth. While another nurse took the little girl and cleaned her up, the doctor assisted as the second little girl, fussing with outrage, slid out into his waiting arms.

Taylor was too busy to do anything but laugh and cry at the same time as she watched Brett cut both cords. Brett bent over both girls and then returned to Taylor's bedside, her face awash with tears. "I can't believe how perfect they are. I love you so much. God, Taylor, you are amazing."

Brett burst into fresh tears as she hugged Taylor tightly in her arms. The two women held each other for a short time before the doctor interrupted them.

"Taylor, we need to take the babies and have them weighed, measured, and checked out. We also need to take care of you. I suggest that Brett go out and let everyone know about your beautiful children. We'll get you cleaned up and then let you sleep for a little bit. This will probably be the last sleep you get for many months."

"Okay, Doctor, is Taylor okay?"

"She's fine, Brett. So are your girls."

"Thanks so much."

"You're very welcome."

"Honey, go. I'll be fine." Taylor kissed Brett and then gently pushed her toward the door. Her eyes stayed on Brett until the door shut behind her and then she lay back on the bed, exhausted from the long labor and delivery. It had been a long twenty hours, and she was terribly tired.

"Taylor, how are you doing?"

"Tired, more than anything."

"I used a local so you won't feel any pain. I need to put in a couple of stitches, and then we'll clean you up and let you sleep. Your children will be brought back in an hour or so."

"Are they really okay?"

"They looked perfect to me, a little small but very feisty."

"Will you tell Brett to come back inside when you're done?"

"I will."

CHAPTER 24

▼

An hour later, Taylor's eyes fluttered open to find Brett sitting quietly beside her bed watching her sleep. "Honey, how are the babies?"

"Excellent, the nurses say they're in good health. Rose is six pounds two ounces, and Jane is five pounds eight ounces." Taylor and Brett had decided to name their girls after both of their mothers. "How are you doing?"

"Good—I feel pretty good right now. Can I see the babies?"

"Sure. The nurse brought a wheelchair for you, and I can wheel you over to the nursery. They were sleeping when I visited them a little while ago."

"Has everyone else seen them?"

"Yep, Jeb cried and so did Fran. I finally convinced all of them to go home and get some sleep."

"How are you, honey?"

Brett smiled and bent over placing her face close to Taylor's. "I can't remember ever feeling this good. My life just keeps getting better and better. I love you and our babies. They're so damn beautiful, with a little bit of dark red hair the same color as their mother's."

"I love you, Brett. I'm so proud of you. You showed everyone in Italy what it takes to be a world-class athlete. Your mother would be so proud."

"She would be been even prouder of our children."

"Her grandchildren."

"Yes, she would have been a fantastic grandmother."

"We've got Helen and Fran."

"You're forgetting Jeb and Rex."

"Our family, it's so perfect, so magical. I love you."

"I love you." Are you ready to see our girls?"

"One more thing and then I will be."

"What's that honey?"

"Will you kiss me? I've missed you so much I just need you to hold me for a minute."

Brett crawled up on the bed next to Taylor bed and wrapped her arms around her. Then she bent her head and kissed Taylor gently, slowly, her heart bursting with love. She held Taylor for quite a while because Taylor slid back into a contented sleep with Brett's arms wrapped securely around her.

Their girls were brought back to the room in bassinets before Taylor woke up. Brett was still next to her, her eyes on the two sleeping children.

"Mom, you were right. There's nothing that can compare with having your own child. I wish you were here to see how beautiful they are. I miss you every day, but I feel you watching over us. I finally got you a gold medal. Thank you for your friendship. I hope I'm half the mother you were to me."

Taylor had awoken in time to hear Brett speak to her mother, and she couldn't keep from crying as she responded. "You're going to be a wonderful mother for our girls. You'll teach them how to love, how to work toward a goal, and how to be a good person. I'm so proud of you, Brett."

"I think you having our children is so much more important than any medal. Do you want to see your girls?" Brett kissed Taylor gently.

"Can we hold them?"

"The nurse said we could. She said you could start breastfeeding them when you felt comfortable."

"No time like the present." Taylor moved to sit up as Brett slid off of the bed. "Why don't you bring me one of them and you hold the other one?"

"Okay, but I've never picked up a baby before." Brett looked scared to death as she slowly slid her hands underneath Rose. "Hey, Rose, are you ready to meet your mother?"

After placing Rose in Taylor's arms, she went back for Jane who was fussing in her bassinet. "Hello Jane, welcome to our family."

Brett turned and her smile was from ear to ear as she looked at Taylor with Rose in her arms. "Well, I guess we won't be getting any sleep for awhile."

"Probably not for eighteen years or so," Taylor laughed as she prepared to feed her little girl.

"I love you, Taylor."

"And I adore you."

CHAPTER 25

▼

Four years later ...

Taylor pulled up in front of the Boulder airport in time to see Jeb striding out of the entrance. She waved to get his attention as she stepped out of her SUV.

"Taylor, you look fantastic." Jeb remarked as he grinned at his best friend and business partner.

Taylor was attired in a pair of forest green ski pants and a lamb's wool jacket, her feet snug and warm in fur lined leather boots. She looked right at home in the snow-covered town of Boulder. It was the dead of winter and icy cold, with snow flurries that had lasted all day long adding to the six inches of compacted snow already on the ground.

"Thanks, Jeb, so do you. I'm so glad you decided to come for a visit." Taylor smiled up at the handsome man as she reached up to hug him. He was wearing slate grey ski pants and a darker grey wool coat.

"So am I. How are my godchildren? Have they recovered from their two weeks in Austria?" Jeb asked as he kissed Taylor on the cheek.

"Yes, but Brett and I haven't. What made us think taking two four-year-old children to the World Cup in Austria was a good idea. They had a blast, but Brett and I are exhausted. The girls are perfect, and they loved the trip. I thought we could drive by the slopes and let you see them in action. Brett's teaching them to ski."

"Are you kidding me?" Jeb looked shocked. They were only four years old and both were extremely smart, but skiing?

"No, and I think Rose is just like her other mother. She's going to tear up the slopes. She has no fear. Jane is a little more controlled, but her style is perfect. They've been skiing with Brett for almost a year."

"Is Brett skiing?"

"Only with the girls, and she's very careful. She doesn't want to take any chances with her knees. One injury could mean another knee replacement. She still skis so beautifully. I love to watch her."

"You love everything Brett does," Jeb chuckled. "The spa is doing very well. I can't believe how much business we're getting. Having a successful U.S. ski coach promoting our spa doesn't exactly hurt."

"We have to turn away clients in Boulder," Taylor responded with a grin of her own. Their business couldn't have been more successful. Taylor and Jeb's business had improved upon its already stellar reputation and now included many international athletes taking advantage of the strong programs and rehabilitation services.

"Maybe we should think of another location," Jeb suggested as he climbed into Taylor's Range Rover.

"Are you serious?" Taylor looked at him with surprise as she started the car. This was news to her.

"Well, I think by the time I'm ready to retire, your daughters will be old enough to run the business," Jeb responded with a big smile.

Taylor grinned at her best friend and business partner. "Maybe Jane, but I think Rose is going to break some hearts on the World Cup ski circuit for awhile. She's so much like Brett it's amazing. Her mannerisms are the same, she has that touch of arrogance that Brett has, and she is downright stubborn. Jane is the businesswoman. You should see her negotiate her allowance. It's like dealing with an MBA; she has her argument prepared before she even asks us for more money." Jeb could hear the pride in Taylor's voice.

"Like mother, like daughter. How are you and Brett doing?"

Taylor sighed happily. "Life just gets better and better. A day doesn't go by that she doesn't show me in some small way how much she loves me. I count my blessings every day that we found each other again."

"You two were made for each other."

"Yes, we were, not that she doesn't drive me crazy some times. She's on a kick to take a family vacation to Australia after this ski season, and she won't take no for an answer. She and the girls have it all mapped out."

"What's wrong with that?"

"Two four year olds who want to see great white sharks, what do you think?" Taylor snorted as she negotiated the short distance from the airport to the ski resort and pulled into the parking lot. "We'll have to walk from here. They're over on the intermediate hill."

"At four—I've got to see this!" Jeb followed Taylor's slim form as she moved quickly across the packed snow. "Hold up! I'm not used to walking in this stuff."

Taylor turned and laughed at Jeb. "At least you dressed appropriately this time."

"Boulder, Colorado, in the middle of winter—of course I'm going to dress for snow." Jeb responded with indignation. The last time he had visited, Boulder had been hit with an unexpected snowstorm. Jeb had been wearing a business suit and loafers with a light overcoat that afforded little protection from the snow and cold. Brett and Taylor had teased him unmercifully before taking him to a local store to get appropriate winter clothes.

"There they are up at the top just getting ready for a run." Taylor shielded her eyes from the bright sun as she watched her lover and her twin daughters begin their run down the mountain. They were a beautiful sight to watch in contrasting parkas and black ski pants.

"How do you know that's them?"

"I'd know Brett anywhere. I also can tell by their pants and parkas." Taylor smiled as she watched her partner and lover elegantly ski down the slope with their two daughters. She fell in love with Brett all over again as she watched her glide effortlessly down the hill.

"My God, they *are* wonderful skiers!"

"They are, and Brett is very patient with them." Taylor's eyes were on Brett's athletic body as she expertly worked her way down the mountain. Her moves looked effortless, Brett's love for skiing evident on her smiling face. Taylor's heart beat faster as she watched her ski.

"God, I just love watching Brett ski."

"She is something. But look at your daughters, and they're so little!"

Brett finally noticed the two spectators as she approached the bottom of the slope. She skied over and stopped in front of Taylor and Jeb, both daughters easily keeping up with her.

"Hey, Mom, did you see us?" Jane asked excitedly.

"I did. You both looked terrific."

"Rose went off the jump even though Mom Brett said no."

"Jane, it's not nice to tattle," Taylor admonished her daughter. Rose's face showed a total lack of contrition as she waited for her mother to express her disappointment in her behavior. But Taylor didn't say a word to her mutinous daughter.

"I just tried it once and Mom Brett already told me how dangerous it was."

"Good, then I don't have to say another word, do I?" Taylor almost laughed out loud as she saw the look of surprise on her daughter's face. Rose was always pushing everyone's patience to the limit. *No* didn't stop Rose when she wanted to do something. She was an extremely trying child for both Brett and Taylor to parent, yet they loved her dearly.

Brett reached out and clasped Taylor's hand in hers in a show of faith and support. "We were just finishing up here. Want us to meet you at home?"

"I thought we could all go get some lunch together. What do you think girls?"

"Yeah, with Uncle Jeb?"

"Yes." Both girls loved Rex and Jeb to death. They began to unhook their skis.

"Okay, then let's stow your gear in the car." Brett began to remove her skis.

"Hey girls, how was Austria?" Jeb asked as both twins began to jabber at once. They had obviously had a great time and competed at telling him about it. He couldn't believe how beautiful the two young girls were. They looked just like their mothers.

"Brett, you looked beautiful skiing down the mountain. You took my breath away." Taylor spoke softly, just for her partner of almost eight years.

"Just looking at you does that to me," Brett remarked, her dark eyes full of passion for the woman she loved. "I love you."

"It's magic isn't it? Every day feels like magic with you, the girls, our life."

"Yes it does. It's magic every morning I wake up with you and magic when we go to bed together at night. In fact, it's a totally magical life day after day and year after year. And the magic will last a lifetime."

Taylor reached out and clasped Brett's hand in hers as she looked over at their two daughters who were teasing Jeb. Both of their daughters had red hair just like their mother. Rose had green eyes and Jane the aquamarine eyes of Taylor's. They were beautiful girls, smart, fun, and healthy. Brett squeezed Taylor's fingers as she followed her gaze to their children. Magic, that's what it was—pure and simple magic.

The End

978-0-595-42899-1
0-595-42899-1

Printed in the United States
74904LV00006B/85-132